We Love Anderson Cooper

We Love Anderson Cooper

Short Stories

R.L. Maizes

CELADON
BOOKS

NEW YORK

WE LOVE ANDERSON COOPER. Copyright © 2019 by R.L. Maizes. All rights reserved. Printed in the United States of America. For information, address Celadon Books, a Division of Macmillan Publishers, 120 Broadway, New York, NY 10271.

www.celadonbooks.com

These stories, or earlier versions of them, first appeared as follows: "Collections" in *Witness;* "Tattoo" in *Bellevue Literary Review;* "L'Chaim" in *MonkeyBicycle;* "A Cat Called Grievous" in *Electric Literature;* "Better Homes and Gardens" (then titled "Mama Jane's Pizza") in *Brain, Child Magazine;* "Couch" in *Blackbird;* "Yiddish Lessons" in *The MacGuffin.* An earlier version of "The Infidelity of Judah Maccabee" originally aired on NPR's *Hanukkah Lights.*

ISBN 978-1-250-30407-0 (hardcover)
ISBN 978-1-250-30409-4 (ebook)
ISBN 978-1-250-30408-7 (trade paperback)

Our books may be purchased in bulk for promotional, educational, or business use. Please contact your local bookseller or the Macmillan Corporate and Premium Sales Department at 1-800-221-7945, extension 5442, or by email at MacmillanSpecialMarkets@macmillan.com.

First Celadon Books Paperback Edition: June 2020

10 9 8 7 6 5 4 3 2 1

For Steve

Contents

~~~~~~~~~~~~~~~~

We Love Anderson Cooper

~~~~~~~~~~~~~~~~
~~~~~~~~

Markus hadn't had sex with Gavin. Not yet. But he couldn't help thinking about it as he lay on his bed, listening through a single earbud to Rabbi Margolin's nasal recording of Leviticus, Chapter 20, Verse 13. "If a man lies with a man . . . both have committed an abomination; they shall be put to death." It was part of Markus's bar mitzvah reading. In less than a month, he was supposed to chant those words from memory in a Cedarhurst, Long Island, temple.

Markus hadn't bothered with the second earbud because he didn't need to hear the recording in stereo to know he hated Leviticus. He didn't need to hear it at all. He swiped the file containing the Torah portion and deleted it. Just like that, the offending words were gone. He breathed easily, the air in his room suddenly light and abundant, his heart full and calm. On a poster above his dresser, Mets' slugger David Wright leaned over home plate, gripping a bat. Markus imagined hitting a home run and the crowd cheering.

His mother, Miriam, was in her study. She wore a short-sleeved sweater tucked into pressed khaki pants and peered at documents open on two computer screens. She had been promoted to vice president at her consulting firm that spring. Less than five feet tall, she nevertheless frightened those who crossed her.

Markus stood in the doorway. "Mom?"

"Yes?" she said, keeping her eyes on the documents.

He would tell her everything if she turned around. Why should he keep his relationship with Gavin a secret? Hadn't she exclaimed, "It's about time," when the Supreme Court legalized gay marriage? Hadn't she worn a pride pin to the wedding of a lesbian cousin?

After he told her, they would tell his dad, who would cry because he cried at everything, especially happy endings. His mom would open a bottle of champagne and say how proud they were of him for having the courage to be himself.

"Yes?" she repeated.

He couldn't say it to her back.

She was busy. Markus had overheard her say to his father the night before, "I don't know how I'll get it all done, with Markus's bar mitzvah and this project deadline coming up." She sat on the boards of three charities.

"Do you need something?" she asked, still facing the screens.

"I accidentally deleted the rabbi's recording."

"How come you never accidentally delete Lil Wayne? I'll e-mail you a backup."

⁓⁓⁓⁓⁓

The next morning, he tried again to tell his mother. "I can't read Leviticus."

His mother was late for work. He followed her through the house as she stuffed her laptop into a messenger bag and pulled on a navy jacket and heels that stabbed the carpet, leaving a bloodless trail. "If you practice, you'll get it."

"No—I can't say the stuff about gays." He wanted her to ask why he couldn't say it. If she did, he would tell her. But if she didn't ask—his mother, who asked a million questions about everything—if she didn't ask, it was because she didn't want to know.

"Don't take it literally," she said, staring at the entryway mirror as she applied plum lipstick.

"How else can I take it?"

"Tell yourself you don't mean it. Or tell yourself you mean the opposite." She kissed the air in front of his forehead and hurried out the door, calling over her shoulder, "Don't forget your lunch."

Furious, he trolled the temple's website that afternoon under an account he created for the purpose—Kosher Fag—leaving comments like *God loves gays* and *Moses was queer*. God's Watching replied, *It's Adam and Eve, faggot,* and *Sodomites burn in hell.* The temple blocked both accounts.

"I don't want a bar mitzvah," Markus announced at dinner. "Dad's not even Jewish."

"Your dad wants you to have a bar mitzvah," his mother said, though his father was sitting right there. "Don't you, Fritz?"

Markus's father cleared his throat. Sawdust clung to his unruly eyebrows. Markus had heard him planing boards in his workshop before dinner. He towered over the kitchen table, which he had built to suit his wife. "I want whatever you and Markus want."

Over the years, the temple congregation had become more progressive, but the rabbi remained a zealot. Markus couldn't remember his father ever attending services, though he occasionally picked up Markus outside after Hebrew school.

"Your father's welcome in temple, if that's what you're worried about," his mother said.

~~~~~~~~~~

With the bar mitzvah two weeks away, Markus was miserable. Even thinking about the Mets-themed party his parents were throwing for him Saturday night after the service failed to cheer him up. He lay on Gavin's bed, his head on his boyfriend's stomach, his heart aching as if he had taken a punch to the chest, and decided once and for all he wouldn't read Leviticus.

Gavin's parents were working late. The rapper Drake stared from a paisley hoodie in a poster pinned above the headboard. Jay-Z's "Fuck With Me You Know I Got It" blasted from desktop speakers.

Gavin was a popular boy whose habit of wearing untucked Oxford shirts, the last button undone, had been adopted throughout the seventh grade. Outside school, he wore headphones and crossed against lights, oblivious to honking horns and ambulance sirens. He was a foot taller than Markus. For years, girls had been including Gavin in their trips to the mall and ice skating. Lately he joined them at concerts, though Markus complained of being left out. No girl ever asked Markus anywhere, and boys never picked him to captain a team. Since Gavin kissed him behind the 7-Eleven six months ago, Gavin's lips cold and tasting like raspberry Slurpee, Markus tried to tell himself he didn't care about his own lesser popularity. He'd been chosen by the only boy who mattered.

Markus had first suspected Gavin was gay when he saw him at their neighborhood community center, loitering outside the room where PFLAG was running a support group for queer kids. Neither boy had the courage to go in, but when they ran into each other at the 7-Eleven a few weeks later, Gavin had motioned for Markus to follow him around back.

"I'm not going to recite the Torah," Markus said now.

"The what?" Gavin was Catholic.

"Leviticus," Markus said. "Fags are 'an abomination.' I told you."

Gavin nodded, but Markus didn't know if he was nodding to the music or because he was following what Markus was saying.

"Remember the valedictorian who came out in his graduation speech? His video was downloaded two million times," Markus said. "That's what I'm going to do in temple."

Gavin sat up abruptly, forcing Markus's head off his stomach. "You're not going to mention me, are you? My father would kill me."

"I won't mention you."

"Don't even say you have a boyfriend."

Markus wished they could come out together. Not only would they get to be themselves, in public, but having Gavin as his boyfriend would be a social triumph. No one would ever exclude him again. "I won't. It'll be fine. I promise."

Gavin let out a breath. "You'll be famous. Everyone will be talking about you."

Markus pictured kids at school congratulating him on his newfound celebrity.

Gavin wound his fingers in Markus's hair, tugging gently on the black curls. Markus's scalp warmed. He felt pleasantly dizzy.

"More guys our age should come out," Gavin said. "I'd like to know who they are."

Markus stared at the luminescent stars glowing dimly on the ceiling. He didn't like the idea of Gavin with other guys.

Gavin pulled Markus on top of him. Even fully clothed, Markus felt as if they were one boy. They moved against each other, and Gavin found Markus's mouth and rapped Jay-Z's song into it.

When Gavin tried to unbutton Markus's shirt, Markus brushed his hand away. It had been like that since the beginning, Markus content to make out, Gavin pushing for more. Markus knew he would eventually give in, but the idea scared him. He wasn't proud of his body the way he knew Gavin must be. He was short and doughy, and though Gavin had seen him in his bathing suit, it would be different if they were having sex. He hated the idea of disappointing Gavin.

In his room later, Markus had second thoughts about surprising his parents with an announcement in temple. His father fried schnitzel—Markus's favorite—every Sunday night. The dusky smell of the sizzling meat almost made up for having to return to school on Monday. A math professor, his father came from a long line of cabinetmakers. He taught Markus to build tables and desks using dovetail joints, handing him a fresh piece of wood without recrimination when Markus missed a cut or cracked a pin, applying too much force in his impatience to join the boards. And his mother: She had written an absence note after he skipped school to attend the Mets' opening day. She helped him with book reports, improving what he wrote with her own views on *The Basketball Diaries* and *The House on Mango Street*. Together his parents attended all of his soccer and baseball games, though coaches often forgot him on the bench.

But Markus was afraid if he told them, his parents would try to stop him from coming out in temple. His mother was secretary of the synagogue's Hadassah chapter, whose members took it upon themselves to enforce decorum in the sanctuary. If he told his father, his father would tell Markus's mother, so Markus couldn't tell his father, either. Markus imagined taking a picture of himself in a rainbow Mets jersey in the photo booth at his party. He envisioned other boys finding the courage to come out at the party and all of them dancing together. He kept his mouth shut.

~~~~~~~~

It was a warm May morning. In his bedroom, Markus struggled to button his white dress shirt, his fingers sweating and wobbly. His father knotted Markus's tie, while his mother ran a lint brush over his pristine navy suit jacket for a third time before handing it to him. When Markus was dressed, his father wrapped an arm around his mother's waist, and they leaned into each other and observed him, a boy they thought they knew.

His mother handed him a folded copy of the speech she had written for him and cleared with the rabbi and the youth director. The speech was about being a member of the Jewish community. Markus didn't plan to read it. He had written something for himself that was about belonging to a different community. It was in the top drawer of his dresser, buried beneath a pile of tube socks. He had memorized it, but planned to bring it anyway, just in case.

His father took out his phone to snap Markus's picture. Markus could tell how proud his parents were, how excited their only child would be honored in the temple, and he knew the day wouldn't go as they expected. Wiping his palms on his pants, he forced a smile.

Two hours later, standing on a stool behind the lectern, Markus smelled bodies pressed too close together, Rabbi Margolin's musk aftershave, and the slow disintegration of parchment Torah scrolls lined up in the ark behind him. Soft light filtered through abstract stained-glass windows just below the ceiling. The temple seats were covered with purple velvet and spring loaded. When he attended services, Markus half expected to find a bucket of popcorn between his knees.

The rabbi rested a hand on Markus's shoulder as he introduced him to the congregation, but Markus wasn't listening. He was picturing a makeup artist preparing him for a morning show, just one of the many TV spots he imagined he would do after the video of his bar mitzvah speech went viral. The valedictorian who came out had appeared on the *Today Show* and CNN. And then there was Sam Horowitz from Dallas. The video of his bar mitzvah dance routine landed him on *Ellen*. After he was famous, Markus thought he might do one of those "It Gets Better" videos that gave hope to gay kids.

He looked down at his mother in the front row. She was smiling, displaying teeth whitened for the occasion. She held one of the dozens of small cellophane bags stuffed with candy she had distributed among the congregation to throw at Markus at the conclusion of the service. Next to his mother sat his father, a silver skullcap perched on his head like a miniature alien craft. At his father's right was Markus's grandmother, Helga, who had flown in from Hamburg. Knowing he was about to disturb a Lifecycle Event, as the Hadassah ladies liked to refer to the bar mitzvah, Markus's legs trembled. He clutched the lectern. He hoped his parents would understand that confronted with Leviticus, he had to be honest about who he was.

In the second row, Markus's classmates from Hebrew school and Martin Luther King Jr. Middle School gazed down at silenced phones, texting or playing World of Warcraft, as he had done during so many interminable bar mitzvahs. Markus located Gavin, whose cheeks were pink—whether from warmth or excitement, Markus couldn't tell. A pale blue shirt fell easily across Gavin's chest. Mindful of his promise not to mention his boyfriend, Markus looked away.

The rabbi droned on, throwing out worn phrases Markus heard at every bar mitzvah: "upstanding young man," "future of the Jewish people," "honor thy father and mother." The man seemed to have a boilerplate speech into which he plugged each boy's name. Perhaps after Markus's announcement, the rabbi would talk about diversity, a subject Markus couldn't remember him ever addressing.

Markus fingered the speech in his pocket his mother had written. "Never be afraid to take initiative," his father had once said to him. "That's what makes a leader," his mother added, only half listening as she bent over her laptop. He was taking that advice now, but he knew they might not see it that way.

The rabbi squeezed his shoulder and receded from the lectern. In the packed synagogue, Markus stood alone.

The congregation stared at him, hundreds of faces shimmering in the heat, flesh pixelating into swaths of pink and yellow and gray. Markus struggled to breathe the thick air. In the back someone coughed, and it startled him. His mouth was as dry as soda crackers, and his tie choked him.

He cleared his throat. Glancing at his mother, her posture erect and her expression a mix of joy and anticipation as she held his father's hand, Markus considered giving the speech she had written. He wasn't responsible for Leviticus, which Jews had been reading in temple for thousands of years. But then he looked at Gavin. Why shouldn't everyone accept him as Gavin had? And why shouldn't he be famous, more popular even than his friend? Markus left his mother's speech in his pocket. A tremor in his voice, he began: "Thank you all for coming to my bar mitzvah."

"Louder," the rabbi stage-whispered from his thronelike chair facing the congregation.

"Remember the people in the back," his mother said.

Markus raised his voice. "The Torah portion of the week is Leviticus."

"Louder," Rabbi Margolin said.

"Project," his mother said. "Like we practiced."

Markus shouted: "In Leviticus . . . In Leviticus—"

"Leviticus—we got it," said the rabbi.

Words that had come easily as Markus practiced them alone in his room now eluded him. He began again. "Things . . . things are different now. People are different."

"Yes?" the rabbi said. But Markus didn't know where to go from there. He reached for his speech, patting his pockets, but found only his mother's. He had forgotten to bring his own.

The congregants leaned toward him, waiting, but Markus's mind remained blank. He felt as exposed as the carvings of Adam and Eve hanging on the wall. Unsteady on the stool, he shifted his feet.

His mother rifled through her large Chanel purse. She pulled out a sheaf of papers, her speech, and waved them. "Markus."

Determined to ignore her for once, he tried again. "Michael Sam," he pleaded. "After he came out, no one in the NFL wanted him. He wasn't drafted until the seventh round. He kissed his boyfriend on TV. On TV!" He didn't know what point he was trying to make.

Markus's mother stopped smiling.

His father cocked his head, sending his silver skullcap to the floor.

His classmates looked up from their phones, the disaster unfolding before them more interesting than the fiery explosions on their screens.

"I didn't even want a bar mitzvah," Markus shouted, but that wasn't what he meant, either.

Clenching his fists, the rabbi stormed over. Still waving her speech, his mother hurried toward him. They were closing in. His time was running out.

"Markus Grunewald, that will be enough," the rabbi said, clutching Markus's sleeve.

"I'm not an abomination," Markus shouted. "Gavin and I are not an abomination." As soon as the words were out of his mouth, he didn't feel quite so alone, but he also couldn't believe what he'd done.

Kids turned to stare at Gavin, who sat there wide-eyed, shaking his head as if it were all a lie.

Veins throbbing at his temples, the rabbi dragged Markus from the lectern. "This is not a church where you make your confessions," he mumbled.

"Michael Sam got a raw deal!" a boy in the second row called out.

"They can't force you to have a bar mitzvah!" came a woman's voice from the back.

"Obama Nation!" shouted the rabbi's young son.

Someone hurled a bag of candy at the rabbi, knocking off his skullcap. Someone else pelted the microphone, which let out a sharp wail.

~~~~~~~~~~

Markus's parents ushered him out of the synagogue. He didn't even have a chance to apologize to Gavin, who huddled in a corner with

Joey Moskowitz, Markus's classmate from Hebrew school. Gavin didn't turn around when Markus called his name.

In the back of his father's Mercedes, Markus slouched next to his grandmother. She rested her tiny, dry hand on his damp one as they drove home.

From the front passenger seat, his mother turned to face him. She ran her fingers through gold hair, wrecking a stylist's careful work. "Why didn't you talk to us first? We would have understood. We love Anderson Cooper. You didn't have to tell us so . . . so . . ."

"Publicly?"

"Yes."

"I tried to tell you. Anyway, if you're not ashamed, why do you care that I told the whole temple?" Markus yanked his shirt from his pants and undid the bottom button.

"It's the kind of thing you tell your parents first, before you announce it to the world."

"Why?"

"So we can protect you."

"What your mother's trying to say is that you can tell us anything," his father said, glancing over his shoulder.

"As long as I do it privately and not in temple and don't tell anyone else unless it's that I made honor roll."

"That's not what we're saying," his father said.

They were quiet for a while, and then his father asked, "Did Gavin know you were going to mention him?"

"It just slipped out."

His mother fanned her face with the speech she had written. "Oy." Markus thought if he could read her mind, she would be imagining him reciting her speech, and the rabbi pumping his hand, not pulling him from the lectern. "You'll have to apologize to Gavin," she said.

"I know."

Markus's dreams of celebrity were already fading. Even if the videographer had captured the events at the temple, it wasn't anything Markus would want to post online. Gavin wouldn't want it publicized, either. Of course, one of his classmates might have gotten it. Markus checked his phone to see if anyone had uploaded a video. He was relieved—and a bit disappointed—not to find one.

Outside the car window, people went about their normal Saturday lives. A postal worker in shorts delivered mail. Young girls in ponytails jumped rope. A boy a grade below Markus rode his bike past their car and Markus wished to trade places with the kid who might never have a bar mitzvah and certainly not one like Markus's.

"My uncle Dieter was gay," his grandmother said in her heavy German accent. Everyone turned toward her except Markus's father, who was driving and looked at her in the rearview mirror.

"Great-uncle Dieter?" his father said.

"Don't sound so surprised. You thought Albert was his friend?"

"That's what he said."

"When the Nazis were in power, Dieter was terrified they would be discovered. Many of their homosexual friends died in camps."

Now his father turned around. "You never said anything."

"Watch the road. We didn't talk about it."

Thinking about his own lack of discretion, Markus felt ashamed. He imagined Gavin's father kicking him out of the house. The Internet was full of stories of homeless gay kids, panhandling or trading sex for money. He and Gavin had read the stories together, never thinking it could happen to them. Even if Gavin's parents didn't throw him out, they might refuse to let him see Markus. Gavin might not *want* to see him after what he'd done. Markus texted Gavin that he was sorry, that it had been an accident. Gavin didn't reply.

Markus continued to text Gavin all afternoon, apologizing and asking him to come over. He finally gave up, figuring he would see him that night. Despite everything that had happened, Markus's mother said they would go ahead with the party. She had posted an update on his bar mitzvah website: "Notwithstanding the unorthodox events at temple, tonight's party will be held as scheduled."

In the catering hall, National League pennants hung from the walls. Baseball caps that said "Markus's Big Game" were piled high on a table, and kids grabbed them and put them on. Inflated bats and beach balls designed to look like baseballs filled giant cardboard boxes. Kids bounced the balls off one another's heads and taped them to the ceiling. They mugged in the photo booth. A deejay played hip-hop, and they did their favorite rappers' moves. Markus's father danced with Helga and with Markus's mother. If Markus's friends cared about what had happened at temple, they didn't mention it. The party would have been perfect, if only Gavin were there.

Markus poked his head out the door every five minutes, looking for his boyfriend. He wondered if Gavin still *was* his boyfriend. He texted Gavin until he couldn't bear not getting a response.

He was sitting at a table, staring at his phone, when a kid at the party sent him a link to a YouTube video: images of him stammering, the red-faced rabbi, bags of candy flying in and out of the frame, and a shot of Gavin shaking his head in what could have been denial or disbelief or both. It wasn't a flattering portrait. Markus felt embarrassed, but he was also excited to see himself on screen and to know the video was circulating. It had been viewed only twenty-five times. He hoped more people would watch it.

When Markus returned from a trip to the door, his father asked, "Everything okay?"

"Gavin hates me." He took off the baseball cap and squeezed the bill between his hands.

"Maybe he's not ready to face everybody."

"No one cares that he's gay."

"He doesn't know that."

"I texted him and told him."

"Think you could try to have a good time without him?"

"No."

~~~~~~~~~

As of Sunday morning, only forty people had watched the video. Markus knew he should be grateful, given how embarrassing the video was, but he couldn't help feeling he had missed his only chance to meet Ellen.

Gavin finally replied to Markus's texts early Sunday afternoon and agreed to ride to the beach with him. They met around the corner from Markus's house.

Straddling his bike, wearing swim trunks and sneakers, Gavin stared at the asphalt. His body, which was always moving, hands drumming his pale belly or thighs, was still. Gone was his easy manner that had enveloped Markus, making him feel there was no reason to be anything but himself. Instead, Markus felt regret, dull and heavy, and a longing for the past. He wished Gavin would look at him.

"You shouldn't have said anything," Gavin said.

"I know."

"You said you wouldn't."

"I'm sorry." Markus wondered if any of his neighbors were watching.

"This morning my father played golf with Sam Miller. He told my father about this kid Markus who came out during his bar mitzvah and outed his friend Gavin. He said, 'Isn't your kid named Gavin?' My father told him to go fuck himself, his kid wasn't queer, but he knew it was me."

"What did he do?"

"My father? He didn't do anything. I said, 'I thought you hated gays?' He said, 'Other gays. Not you.'"

Markus realized he was one of those other gays.

"He said, 'Besides, your mother and I aren't stupid. He's always here, you and him behind a locked door, listening to that garbage. What were we supposed to think?'" Gavin kept his head down. "Then my mother started to cry." He pounded his front tire on the street.

Markus didn't know what to say. "I thought the rabbi was going to hit me."

"I wish he had."

Markus winced. "At least we don't have to pretend anymore."

Gavin shrugged. He squeezed his handlebars and looked down the empty street.

As they rode to the beach, Gavin was unusually quiet. When they arrived, they sat on a bench on the boardwalk. Reconstructed after Hurricane Sandy from concrete and plastic wood, the boardwalk looked nothing like the original hardwood structure. Markus and Gavin had pedaled over the new boards more times than Markus could count, their tires humming.

"There's a video," Markus said. He held tight to the bench. "Not too many people have watched it."

Gavin stared at his lap. "Fuck."

The surf scoured the beach, reclaiming broken shells and motionless starfish. Sweat from the vigorous ride rolled down Gavin's chest. He smelled like exertion, like salt, like himself.

Gavin tightened the tie on his trunks. "I hung out with one of your Hebrew school friends yesterday. Kid named Moskowitz."

"Oh yeah?"

Gavin looked out at the water. "He's gay, you know."

"Joey Moskowitz? That kid's a pizza face. What do you want to hang out with him for?"

"He has built-in speakers in his room and everything Jay-Z has ever recorded."

"I don't give a fuck what kind of speakers he has."

A mother and father played with a small boy in a blue swimsuit, digging a hole just beyond the reach of the waves. Markus's parents, too, had brought him to this beach. Markus's father had taken him under the old boardwalk to show him its construction. They swam and his father taught him how to recognize a riptide—a line of floating debris, a change in ocean color.

The father lifted the boy onto his shoulders and carried him into the surf. Gavin jogged toward the water with Markus behind.

They were up to their waists, the waves coming steady and hard. Markus plowed through the water toward Gavin. Water beaded Gavin's neck. The air smelled of decaying seaweed. Before Markus could reach him, a giant wave broke over them, sending them tumbling.

After they swam, they rode to Gavin's house. His parents were at church, but the boys locked the door to his room just to be safe. Gavin stepped out of his suit and Markus followed. Aroused, the boys didn't stop to put on music. They lay on the bed, and Markus took Gavin in his mouth. It was Markus's first time, and he wasn't sure if he was ready. But he wanted to do something for Gavin, something to make up for outing him. Markus's teeth were in the way, and he wondered if he was doing it right. The last thing he wanted was to hurt him. Gavin swelled and hardened against his lips. He pressed his hands against the back of Markus's head, forcing Markus to take all of him. He tasted bitter, a surprise after the sugary sweetness of his mouth.

Markus thought Gavin would reciprocate, but he didn't. After Gavin came, he turned toward the wall and lay still, sleeping or pretending to sleep. Markus got dressed and rode home.

Later that day, Markus built a chest with his father. Hammers, saws, bevels, T-squares, screwdrivers, vices, clamps, and chisels covered the walls of the workshop. New tools hung alongside old, because his father never discarded anything. Safety glasses were lined up, the child-size ones Markus had first worn next to those almost as big as his father's. Markus breathed the familiar smells of cedar planks and wood finishes. His father handed him the dovetail saw.

"Are you mad?" Markus asked, though after spending time with Gavin, he worried less about how his father felt.

"Pay attention when you're making a cut."

After Markus finished, his father took the saw. "We worry people will give you a hard time. We wish you had waited."

Markus examined the cut. Distracted, he had missed the line his father had drawn. "I didn't want to wait to be with Gavin."

"How does Gavin feel?"

"I don't know." Thinking about what he had done with Gavin, Markus blushed. The workshop, which had once felt as big as the house, now seemed too small for him and his father. "Is Mom still upset?"

"She knows you tried to tell her. She wishes she had listened."

"Did I ruin her life?"

"Not her life."

"Just the bar mitzvah."

"Her entire Hadassah chapter was there," said Markus's father. "She may have trouble getting reelected."

"Grandma's probably sorry she came all this way."

"Your grandma's happy for any excuse to see you. And she's been through enough in her life to know that what happened isn't the end of the world."

~~~~~~~~

At school on Monday, Markus overheard his name everywhere kids huddled together. His friends said it was cool he was gay and that Gavin was his boyfriend. They asked if he had seen the video. The number of views had mushroomed to ten thousand. Markus hid in a bathroom stall and refreshed the screen on his phone to watch the counter advance, so excited he nearly dropped the phone into the bowl.

He tried desperately to catch Gavin alone, but every time Gavin saw Markus, he turned his back. Markus wanted to touch Gavin's hand or his face and to tell Gavin how happy he was about what they had done, though in truth, he wasn't sure. Staking out Gavin's locker, he leaned his head against the cold, beige metal and remembered how before the bar mitzvah they had met there and made plans. Gavin never appeared, and Markus was late for class.

At lunch, he searched for him in the cafeteria, toting an empty green tray from table to table and pacing up and down the serving line, where he gagged on odors of warmed-over pizza and fish cakes. When the bell signaled the end of lunch period, he had yet to eat.

Monday afternoon, he finally caught Gavin alone in a hall.

Gavin didn't look happy to see him. "Kids I used to think were my friends are talking behind my back. Girls especially," Gavin said. "You're a hero for coming out. They think I was a tease who pretended to be something I wasn't."

Markus reached for Gavin's arm, but Gavin shook him off. "I didn't mean to out you," Markus said.

"Maybe you did and maybe you didn't." Gavin walked away, his beautiful back receding along the cinder-block wall, a spot of light in an otherwise dim hallway.

During the week, each time Markus checked the video, the number of views climbed, from twenty-five thousand to thirty-five, then fifty. Markus's classmates were giddy. He was becoming the most popular boy in the seventh grade. Girls asked him to sit with them in the cafeteria. Two boys from the lacrosse team invited him over to play video games, and he went, feeling like a stranger.

Everyone loved him except Gavin, who ignored him, refusing to talk to him at school or to reply to the texts Markus sent morning to night. After school on Friday, Markus tried again, texting Gavin that they should ride to the beach.

"Hanging w Joey" came the answer.

"Tell him u got 2 go." Markus waited a minute, and when he

didn't hear back, he texted Gavin that he missed him. After another minute, he begged Gavin to come to his house and talk.

Alone, Markus hurtled toward the temple on his bike. He crashed into potholes and flew over speed bumps, the violent rattle of his bike an echo of what he felt inside. When he arrived he found a rock the size of a walnut with flintlike edges. He walked to the rear of the building, which bordered the congregants' parking lot, empty because it was hours before Friday night services. He knew which was the rabbi's window, having visited the office in preparation for his bar mitzvah. The room was empty and dark. Pressing the rock to the glass, he chiseled in large, uneven letters: *GOD HATES GAYS*. He snapped a picture of the window with his phone. As he ran back to his bike, he tossed the rock. He pedaled home, longing to feel Gavin's weight against him, the tangle of their limbs. The fact that Gavin was probably in Joey's bedroom, his hands in Joey's hair, kissing him or worse, tore at Markus.

~~~~~~~

"It was a mistake to come out," Markus declared at dinner. He reached under the tablecloth and squeezed the edge of the oak dining table his father had built.

His grandmother sat across from him. She smoothed the cloth, her fingers twisted with age. "I once asked Dieter if it was worth it. Couldn't he have lived with a woman? He said his life was better than most people's."

"But Albert never abandoned him," Markus said.

"No."

Markus's father stared at him and then leaned back in his chair, his face sagging.

His mother returned from the kitchen with platters of brisket and steamed green beans. "A cable TV reporter called me this afternoon. She saw the video of the bar mitzvah and wants to interview you."

Markus hadn't been aware his mother even knew about the video. "What did you say?"

"That it was up to you. I just texted you her number."

"She'd probably want to talk about Gavin."

"Yes."

It was what he had wanted, to be famous and impress his friends. But even his brief popularity had worn him out. Being surrounded by classmates only reminded him of who was missing. If he did the interview, it would be hard on Gavin. But if he didn't do it, when Gavin tired of Joey, he might miss Markus and come back to him.

Quiet settled over the table as his father served his grandmother. She was flying back to Hamburg in the morning. Markus would be sorry to see her go.

In his bedroom after dinner, Markus thought about Gavin and Joey. He hoped Gavin got a flat the next time he rode with Joey, and fell and scraped his elbows and soft palms. He hoped Joey's mother discovered her son was gay and cried and smashed his speakers.

Glancing at his phone, Markus saw the video had reached a hundred thousand views. He took a screen shot of the number, more out of habit than interest. For the last time, he erased the rabbi's recording of Leviticus. He had at least managed not to recite it in temple. That might be all he chose to remember about his bar mitzvah service. It would be all he chose to tell. Scrolling through texts, he found the reporter's phone number and deleted it. Then he texted Gavin a picture of the defaced temple window with the caption, "GOD HATES RABBIS." His phone buzzed with the reply.

Collections

~~~~~~~~~~
~~~~~~~~~

Maya lived with Peter for fourteen years without God's or Dade County's blessing. When Peter died, and his three daughters flew in and divided the property—the art, the furnishings, even the clothing—she held back tears until they left, then cried abundantly in the mornings when his death seemed most impossible, a nightmare carried into day.

His ocean-view condo, infinity pool in front and swim-up bar in back, was sold. Maya returned to her rundown Miami bungalow, the floor collapsing beneath her grief because termites had eaten the joists. Sea air pushed through the cracked living-room windows. She covered them with butcher paper, casting a pall over the small room.

She moved back in with few possessions, the adjustable bed she'd shared with Peter that he died in, a rug she'd taken before his children arrived. Small compensation for counting pills and spooning applesauce into a toothless hole.

Maya hired a contractor to repair the floor in the bungalow.

Alberto wasn't a young man, but he combed his hair in the style of the young, applying mousse that appeared as small clouds of white foam against his unnaturally black hair, which he wore long and wrapped behind his ears. His khaki shirt fit snugly.

Sitting at a weathered pine table, spinning the nub of a pencil, Maya reviewed the estimate he had given her. "It costs too much."

"It costs what it costs. You can make payments."

"Make payments with what?"

He looked through the bedroom door and pointed at the adjustable bed with massage settings. "You can give me that."

The couch was a sleeper with springs that complained, but it would do. Alberto got to work pulling up slats in the living-room floor.

Only sixty-five, twenty years younger than Peter, Maya had some beauty left. She was slim and compact with black kinky hair that brushed the small of her back, but she vowed she would never be with another man. It had taken too much out of her to love Peter.

They had met shortly after Peter's wife died when he was looking for someone to cook for him. The extra money appealed to her. She won him over with her fried plantains and rice *con gandules*. The bedroom wasn't far from the kitchen.

She had fallen for his wry, democratic charm, for the way he lifted his trimmed gray eyebrows when she entered a room, as if her very existence was an agreeable surprise. Doormen, shoeshine men asked after Peter. But his personality, like his body, withered after the stroke. Even as she sponged and turned him, her feelings for him never lessened.

Maya received Social Security from her time working in a hospital, making calls to collect bills from people as poor as herself. She had worked there for twenty years, quitting after she moved in with Peter. The government check lasted half the month. Then she joined lines at soup kitchens alongside other retirees who stared hopelessly into orange plastic trays. In the windowless YMCA basement, Maya hid behind oversize sunglasses and mumbled thanks to the servers.

She had forgotten how to live without money, forgotten the racks of expired bread and overripe bananas in the back of the supermarket, and government programs that could pay for her eyeglasses. It seemed unfair to have to learn all that again when learning no longer came easily.

Her time of eating filet mignon and drinking vintage Tuscan wines with Peter was over. She thought often of his airy apartment, his startling art—giant frogs leaping about in one painting, a fat man and woman dancing in another. She had pushed his wheelchair into galleries where he was greeted by name: Mr. Drayson. He pointed to what he liked. The staff overlooked Maya, until Peter asked her opinion. Then they rushed to get her a glass of water to match his, and she observed their confusion over who and what she was. She drank, though she wasn't thirsty, hiding her face behind the glass until her anger passed.

His daughters never visited, not until he was dying. Then they came and cried and read the will and stopped crying.

~~~~~~~~~~

Maya slept fitfully on the couch and woke irritated the next morning. It was not quite seven o'clock when she walked to the Holy Family Catholic Church, passing a check-cashing place and a cell-phone store, metal shutters still down for the night. A barefoot woman curled up in a doorway, likely sleeping but possibly dead.

Afraid to get too close, Maya couldn't tell. The air hung motionless, smelling of the sea and stale garbage.

At church she arranged to have a Mass said for Peter, though he was an atheist. She dropped a dollar in the plate and cursed Peter for not marrying her or at least leaving her something so she wouldn't have to rely on charity. She confessed.

"Anger is a venial sin," the young priest said.

"What if it's justified?"

"Still."

Maya remembered why she rarely went to church. She clutched the narrow shelf in the confessional. "He hid our relationship from his children."

"No good comes from living together without the holy sacrament." The priest spoke quickly, as if a line of parishioners were waiting to confess, but in truth the church was almost empty. No one cared about the poor, not even the priest, who wore Armani shoes and a bright collar.

When she got home, Alberto was working. Only the top of his head showed above the hole he had excavated. Sawdust littered his hair.

"I almost fell in last night." She sat on the couch.

He looked up from the hole. "You wouldn't be the first." Dirt lodged in the wrinkles next to his eyes. His face was as round as a tortilla.

"What about some cones? Like the ones on the highway."

"I'd have to lift them from a construction site."

She rested her head against the wall and contemplated the ceiling paint peeling in husks. "This house needs to be painted."

"You hiring me for another job?"

"I had only one bed." She looked into the empty bedroom.

"What did you do for a living?"

"I collected bills for the hospital."

Alberto scratched his stomach. "I called the hospital once. When my wife was dying. They gave us a payment plan, but they wouldn't cut the bill."

"If it was up to me, I would have cut your bill."

Alberto shook his head. "You say that now. But people like power when they have it."

"Don't hold it against me."

"Maybe you could collect bills for me. I'll give you ten percent. Before you know it, you'll have enough money for painting."

Alone that night, Maya remembered the early years with Peter when he had teeth and his body was capable of pleasing her. Once he took her to a dinner party where waiters in tuxedos served steaming lobster out of the shell. He dipped the flesh in butter and fed it to her, unmindful of sideways looks from other guests. She was excited by his attentions but embarrassed he had introduced her simply as Maya—not *wife*, or *girlfriend*, or even the lesser *friend*. Was it her imagination or did her skin grow darker among that crowd? The other women wore heavy jewels as if unaware of them.

When they returned from dinner, they sat in the living room opposite each other on white leather chairs. Elbows on his knees, Peter stared at the ebony floor and told her how he had worked throughout college as a busboy in an Upper East Side restaurant favored by his Columbia classmates. "You can't imagine the things they left for me to clean up," he whispered.

He rarely spoke of anything but his success. Maya mourned his humiliation but was secretly pleased he shared it with her.

Now she climbed off the worn fabric couch, hands pressed to her stomach. It was the fifteenth of the month. Her Social Security check wouldn't arrive until the twentieth. She brewed a pot of coffee and drank three cups.

The next morning Alberto arrived late, his pallor yellow, his hair in disarray.

"Do you want some coffee?" she asked.

"My wife visited me in my sleep. She hit me with a hammer for cheating on her. I told her when you work in houses where women are home, you are bound to end up in bed with them."

"What did she say?"

"She kept beating me." He seemed reluctant to climb into the hole. "Why don't I measure for painting? Then, if you get some money, you'll know what it costs."

"Measure anything you want."

He extracted a tape measure, a pencil, and a notepad from his toolbox. He put on glasses held together with copper wire and worked out the numbers. After a while—longer than necessary, it seemed—he told her what it would cost.

"Now I know," she said.

"Now you know."

He resumed his work and she heard the electrical saw cutting out diseased wood and smelled sawdust and mud. The hammer tapped in healthy pine joists, which had their own smell, optimistic, like you would expect from something recently alive.

Alberto's notes were on the table, showing the individual room measurements he had taken. But he hadn't factored in the cost of paint or totaled anything. Instead, he had sketched the living room, the paper over the cracked windows and a gaping hole in the floor.

He had drawn her sitting on the couch, a cup of coffee in hand, her hair pinned back (though she was wearing it down) to accentuate her cheekbones. As for the estimate, he'd apparently made it up. She tore the sketch out of his notebook, crumpled it, and threw it in the trash. It was a flattering portrait, but she was tired of men deceiving her.

That afternoon, Alberto finished the foundation and rebuilt the floor with weathered boards the owners of another house had wanted removed. He sanded the surface so Maya wouldn't get splinters. The wood was gray and pocked with small knotholes, rough despite the sanding. Maya couldn't smell it at all. But it was sturdy, and for that she was grateful.

In the kitchen, Alberto lingered over a glass of ice water. He scratched his forehead, licked his lips, and pressed the glass to his cheek. Maya could tell what was coming but didn't encourage it. "Why don't I take you to dinner?" he said.

She agreed because she was hungry. She wished he would take a shower, but he led her straight to his truck.

He opened the passenger door and cleared the front seat of a saw and termite spray. It had been a long time since Maya had hoisted herself into a truck, and blood rushed to her head from the exertion. Peter had a BMW and a driver who opened the door for her.

Alberto drove to a Mexican restaurant nearby. "This was my wife's favorite restaurant."

Maya didn't say anything. Men didn't have any sense of what a woman wanted to hear. Not even Alberto, who wanted to get into every woman's bed.

Above their booth, a yellow bulb flickered in a tin wall sconce. Maya ordered chalupas with beef. When they came, she took a deep breath and a large bite and patted the sides of her mouth to keep the beef from leaking out. It felt good to be sitting opposite a man, even if the man had sawdust in his hair. So many of her meals these days were taken alone or among people she didn't know.

She had ordered the *grande*, so she would have leftovers for the next day. With great effort, she refrained from eating it all. She asked the waitress for another basket of chips and a refill of Coke.

When it came, Alberto lifted his red plastic cup. "To forgetting the dead!"

Maya knew then Alberto's wife had been at the dinner. She raised her cup to be polite.

After the meal, Alberto dropped her at her house. "Can I take you out again?"

She looked at his stained pants and calculated how long it would be before her next Social Security check ran out. "Call me in a few weeks." She planned to dress like a nun.

She swept, mopped the floor, and rolled out the rug. Perhaps she could trade the rug for new windowpanes. She would call Alberto and ask him. And maybe she would do collections for him. People should pay their bills. It wasn't her fault if they didn't have money.

The next day, Maya and Alberto talked, and Alberto brought over a list of clients whose accounts were more than ninety days past due.

"Why don't you have them pay before you do the work?"

"They pay half up front, for materials. They don't want to give me that. They look at me and see a thief."

Maya nodded and sighed. When Peter's daughter Gwendolyn had realized Maya shared Peter's bed, she accused Maya of trying to steal the estate. But later, after Gwendolyn read the will, she took Maya's hands. "We're so grateful for your service," she said, her smile bright and hard. The word *service* clattered around Maya's brain. Light reflecting off Gwendolyn's teeth blinded her. If there had been a theft, Maya had not committed it.

When Alberto left, Maya looked at the list of deadbeat customers and realized she was back where she'd started, except she was older and instead of the hospital to back her up, she had only a *coscolino* like Alberto. In her dreams, Peter continued to pay for groceries with credit cards whose limits were never reached. But in daylight, her pantry was empty. She had always assumed Peter would take care of her, and the fact that he hadn't made her wonder what they had been doing together all those years and whether what felt to her like love to him had felt like—what? It was the kind of thinking that could drive a person crazy.

She waited until evening to phone the first customer on the list.

"Mr. Alexi?"

"Yes?" His voice was calm and put Maya at ease. Perhaps the work would be easier than she expected.

"I'm calling about the tile job Alberto Salazar did for you last spring."

"Who is this?" he demanded.

She straightened her blouse. "My name is Maya. I do collections for Alberto. You owe him six hundred dollars."

"I don't owe that son of a bitch a penny. He slept with my daughter. She's only twenty."

Maya swallowed. "A contract is a contract."

"Who are you? Are you his wife? Why do you let him run around like that?"

"I'm a widow."

"You should work for someone else." He hung up.

Maya crossed his name off the list. She got herself a glass of water and looked at the ceiling. She imagined it smooth and white.

The next call was similar. She reached a man who said Alberto shouldn't be allowed around women. Maya wondered why Alberto hadn't made a pass at *her*. She didn't want to sleep with him, but still.

She made several more calls that evening.

A week later, Alberto came to do the windows. He had already collected the rug. He brought new panes with him.

She told him the collections were not going well. "You should wait to sleep with them until you get paid."

"It would be wrong to plan it. Worse than getting caught up in the moment. Besides, I'm only attractive when I'm working."

It was true. Alberto's nose was long and his torso was short. His face was leathered and covered with spots from working in the sun. But when he worked, and the muscles on his arms and back flexed, and tools whirred and things got fixed, he seemed powerful and appealing.

Peter had never fixed anything. Even when he was younger and stronger, he hired workers. He called the building maintenance man to change light bulbs. He had his business manager hook up the cable TV.

Alberto took down a window frame and set it on the table, which he had covered with brown paper. He hammered out cracked panes and scraped away dried putty.

Maya stretched her toes and wished she could run them through the rug's thick pile. She went into the kitchen to continue the collection calls.

"Mrs. Aguilera? How are you today?"

"No thanks." A television was playing in the background. The woman was at best half listening to Maya.

Maya kicked the table leg. She raised her voice. "I'm not selling anything."

"I'm not interested in taking a survey."

Maya breathed deeply and tried to keep the frustration out of her voice. "I work for Alberto Salazar. He rebuilt your shower last year."

"Oh! Alberto. He did a beautiful job. I couldn't be happier. I'm thinking of having him do more, uh, work for me. Is there a problem?" She lowered the volume on the television.

"It seems the two-thousand-dollar balance on the account was never paid."

"I'm terribly sorry. My husband must have forgotten. I'll put a check in the mail today. I could bring it to his house if he'd like."

"Mail will be fine."

So that was what it would take. She would have to talk to the women. Thinking about it made her feel like she had eaten spoiled empanadas. Nevertheless, she would do it. She drank a cup of black tea and made a few more calls, marking the results on the spreadsheet Alberto had given her.

She rinsed out her cup and went into the living room to observe his progress.

He pressed fresh putty into a window frame and evened it out with his gloved finger before pushing a new pane into place. He nodded at Maya. "Want to try? Then when it breaks again, you'll know how to fix it."

"Is it going to break again?"

"Eventually."

Maya didn't want to fix it. She wanted Peter to call someone. She had changed his diapers, run his food through a blender.

"What's wrong with me?" Maya asked.

Alberto looked up from his work. "There's nothing wrong with you. You're like the Roma tomatoes in my garden. Ripe and firm."

"But you keep your distance."

Alberto took off his safety glasses, wiped his forehead with the back of his sleeve. "You're thinking about someone else. He's always in front of your eyes."

"I can't help it." Beyond a hole in the wall where a window had been, a screaming blue jay chased a sparrow. "I want to kill him."

"He's dead already."

"Did you want to kill your wife?"

"I wanted to kill her while she was dying. She was suffering, and everyone else, my kids, were suffering with her. Then, after she died, I wanted her back even for a few minutes." Alberto began to rehang the window frame with its new panes. "Don't wash them for a week."

The cloudy windows were a disappointment. Maya thought she would have clear windows that day to console her for the loss of the rug. She had almost nothing left of Peter.

That night Maya paced her small house. She resented Alberto for taking her bed and her rug. She had made up the couch but didn't want to get in. She examined Alberto's hammer, which he had forgotten. It was an old hammer, worn at the head, the wood handle discolored. He was not a rich man, though he was richer than she was. Everyone was.

She woke in the middle of the night and called Gwendolyn, who lived in Wisconsin. "I was his wife," Maya said.

"Who is this?" She was half asleep, her voice thick.

"I was his wife." Maya grabbed the hammer.

"You were his housekeeper." Now awake, Gwendolyn sounded resigned, as if she had been waiting for Maya's call and was relieved to finally get it.

"That's what he told you, but I was his wife." The moon appeared as a smudge through her windows.

"His wife was my mother. She died fifteen years ago."

"He took me into his bed."

"Did he marry you?"

"I took care of him." She raised the hammer and considered throwing it through a window if only to see the moon more clearly. But she had given up the rug for the windows. Gwendolyn hung up.

A week later Maya received a letter from Gwendolyn's lawyer. The gold letterhead was raised; the paper was fine and had a watermark Maya puzzled over. The letter warned her not to contact Gwendolyn or any of Peter's children again. The attorney noted that certain items had disappeared from Peter's apartment; the children had ignored the thefts, but their attitudes could change.

Maya crumpled the letter, then straightened it, then crumpled and straightened it again. She put it in the drawer in the kitchen where she kept things she didn't know where to keep. She called Alberto and told him about the letter.

"Don't mess with white people," he said.

"He was my husband."

"I know."

"Do you want to take me out to dinner?"

"Sure."

"I like that Mexican place, but I don't want to hear about your wife."

"Okay. Don't order enough for two days. I'll take you out again if you like."

When he picked her up, he was wearing clean pants.

"Did you work today?" she asked.

"I finished early." He glanced around the room. "The windows look nice."

"I cleaned them with vinegar."

Alberto opened his wallet and handed her a check for two hundred dollars. "Your pay."

As she folded it and put it in her purse, she thought about the mangoes and oranges she would buy. She could already feel the juices running down her chin, the fibers stuck between her teeth.

Tattoo

~~~~~~~~~
~~~~~

Trey knocked hard, and a slim woman wearing a *Mountain Ink* baseball cap came to the locked door of the tattoo shop. She gazed at him through the glass, keeping her expression blank, as polite strangers did. He knew what people saw: bulbous eyes, neck as thick as a bucket, and black moles as large as quarters splattered across his face, climbing into his nostrils and over his eyelids. Only his wife, Nava, didn't seem to mind.

The woman pointed to the hours stenciled on the glass and called out: "Not till noon." Images covered her arm—a red fox, wilting roses, a flaming skull, and the words *Mountain Ink* spilling from a jar of black ink and forming a silhouette of the Rockies. Butterflies froze midflight on her neck.

"Apprentice job," he called back. He scratched his forearm though it didn't itch and tugged at the sleeve of his black T-shirt. It had been two decades since he'd applied for a job.

She opened the door. "I'm Alisande. This is my shop," she said, as she led him over a gray, polished concrete floor to a barber chair. She eyed his hairy arms and pale neck. "You don't have any, do you?"

"No."

"You don't have any ink, but you want to ink other people. Whatever. Have a seat, I guess."

He wanted to say if it was a requirement, he'd get a dozen, but he was afraid to sound desperate, so he kept quiet.

Across the room, designs papered a brick wall and a sign proclaimed, "Tattoos Hurt." Trey hadn't thought about that.

Two other applicants arrived, a man and woman who looked to be in their twenties, with firm skin and full heads of hair, hers short and spiky and unnaturally black, his long and ponytailed. Alisande directed them to a leather couch.

A tiger, an elephant, and a giraffe marched from the young woman's wrist to the shoulder strap of her tank top. On the back of her hand, the door to a small, empty cage hung open. Tribal tattoos stamped the man's neck and showed in the vee of a T-shirt that hugged his narrow, hairless chest. The young woman stared at Trey and then snapped his picture with her cell phone when Alisande's back was turned. Trey's ears grew hot and he went back to examining the wall.

Trey hadn't told Nava the pay was almost nothing, that the apprentice's duties included scrubbing floors and running errands, according to the online ad. As it was, she didn't approve.

"I can teach you how to tattoo, but I can't teach you how to draw," Alisande said, as she passed each applicant a black pen and a sheet of blank paper on a clipboard. "Let's start with a three-dimensional open box."

Trey was first to finish. Alisande walked around evaluating the samples. "Good," she said, when she saw Trey's. He felt a rush of pride and then admonished himself. He had an MFA from the Art Institute of Chicago, for Christ's sake. Never mind that he hadn't sold a painting in months.

"Now an apple on a branch."

Again, Trey finished first. His apple was pink. The leaves, a sun-lit green.

"How'd you get those colors?" Alisande asked.

Holding up the pen, Trey shrugged. He was as surprised as she was. He drew a line, but the ink was black.

"Guy's cheating," the young man muttered.

Alisande looked at his sketch. "I said apple, not Frisbee." Resting the clipboard on his thighs, he tightened his ponytail.

She gave them each a fresh sheet. "Last one: A woman lying on a couch. You have seven minutes."

After three minutes, the young man balled up the paper, pitched it on the floor, and left. At five minutes, Alisande called time. "Take a drawing class," she said to the woman. "Spend a lot of time practicing. Then come back."

She handed Trey a hat like hers. "You need some ink. Somewhere visible. Let's come up with designs this afternoon. I'll tattoo them in the morning."

Back in his truck at the end of the day, Trey pumped his fist.

~~~~~~~~~~~

"You're going to get tattooed for a job you may not have next month?" Nava fished a pack of sugarless gum from her desk drawer. She stuffed two pieces into her mouth and chewed, foil wrappers littering the legal pad and briefs spread before her.

Trey stood in the doorway of her home office, as always intimidated by the thick files on her desk. "She wants to be sure I'm serious." He fanned himself with three sketches he had come to show her. "How would you feel getting a tattoo from someone who didn't have any?"

"You don't have to do this."

"I want to." When his art was selling, Trey didn't care that what he earned barely equaled Nava's bonus. But when canvasses stacked up hopelessly against walls and on tables in his studio, her success magnified his failure and he felt like a burden. Commissions had dried up after he produced an unflattering portrait of the city's new mayor—flesh piling beneath his chin and light bouncing off his scalp through thinning, ash-colored hair. Critics had called his work ugly. But Trey believed his subjects' imperfections reflected their humanity, and what could be more beautiful than that?

Nava shared his aesthetic. It had brought them together fifteen years before in a well-lit Chicago gallery during his only one-man show. She had examined his work close up and from a distance, read his artist's statement, and then viewed the paintings again, finally selecting a portrait of his aging father, skin draping from his neck like a curtain and veins ballooning on his hands. Attracted to her concentrated gaze, Trey was briefly jealous of his own paintings. He talked to her about the history of portraiture, and she smiled when he managed a joke. Listening to her, Trey discovered she was well educated in the arts and her opinions were original. When she looked at his face, he could tell she saw him, not his moles, and that she liked what she saw.

Approaching her desk, Trey said, "I don't mind getting tattooed. It's art people will see."

"All of a sudden skeletons and hearts are art?"

Reluctantly he laid down the drawings. Alisande had sketched an artist's palette dripping paint, forming the word *Trey*. A nude woman with sharp shoulders and large thighs was Trey's work. He had pictured Nava as the model, changing details—the length of the nose, the distance between the eyes—to avoid embarrassing her. Alisande had advised him that nude tattoos weren't popular anymore, but the human body was what he knew best. Lester, the other tattoo artist in the shop, had drawn a tattoo gun in a cartoon style.

Nava spit her gum into a wrapper and dropped it into the trash. "I like the nude."

~~~~~~~

Alisande started him with simple designs: anchors, bows, and crosses. He missed the isolation of his studio. Lester chattered endlessly above the shop's mix of heavy metal, hip-hop, and classical music. As Trey consulted with Alisande about each tattoo, clients stole looks at his face. Still, he was learning a craft, which gave him a sense of hope and possibility, things he hadn't felt in a long time.

He struggled to work on flesh, which was full of irregularities and had more give than stretched linen canvas. As he stitched images into their skin, clients winced. Alisande instructed him never to apologize, only to ask if they wanted to continue.

He progressed to cobras, openmouthed and ready to strike, and clematis and silver bells on vines.

"I'm Melanie and this is Grace," a client said to Trey, as she showed him a picture of her infant daughter. The child had her mother's eyes, large and the color of a pale sky. "Two and a half pounds when she was born. But look at her now. She keeps outgrowing her onesies." Melanie pointed to her bicep. "I want an angel to celebrate."

Trey sketched a winged child with pastel eyes and transferred the image to Melanie's skin. As he dipped the needle in ink, he steadied himself. Every moment was ripe for a mistake—a crooked outline, a muddy shadow. He drew the black lines slowly. To fill in pink cheeks and gold wings, he moved the needle in small, tight circles.

Two hours later the angel was complete. Melanie squeezed Trey's gloved hand. "Now I can never lose her," she said, her breath ragged. For the first time, Trey understood the power of his new art.

Trey's colors were more vibrant than Alisande's or Lester's, though they came from the same suppliers. His lines hovered above the skin. Looking at his images, people forgot they were looking at tattoos. When he inked an alligator, swamp water dripped from their skin, and when he tattooed a rose, they smelled its perfume.

Word of Trey's style spread after *Inked* magazine ran one of his nude tattoos on the cover under the headline, "Fine Artist Turns to Ink." The nude was a woman with thin arms and a wrinkled forehead. Trey watched Nava trace the magazine image with her finger, nodding. She was sitting on the living room couch and didn't seem to notice him.

Stepping into the kitchen, he rested his back against the stainless-steel refrigerator and sighed, relieved she had found something in the tattoo to admire.

But she didn't mention the magazine during dinner.

In bed that night, he kissed her breastbone. "I'm going to tattoo you."

"I don't think so. It wouldn't go with a suit."

"You don't always wear a suit."

〰〰〰〰〰

Customers sought Trey out. They reviewed his portfolio and waited for him, even if Alisande or Lester were free. On first seeing Trey, some were taken aback, but remembering his work, their expressions softened. Trey's confidence grew. He stopped lowering the bill of his cap to hide his face.

One afternoon, Melanie returned to the shop. Her head was wrapped in a lemon-colored scarf and her cheeks were hollow. "Will you do my nipples?" she asked. The doctors had caught her cancer in time. But the surgeons left her with reconstructed breasts "like sightless eyes." She clutched the back of a tattoo chair. "When my husband sees nipples, he'll forget I was sick."

Nipples weren't part of Trey's plan. But tattoos hadn't been, either. He led her to a back room and mixed colors against her skin, blending pinks, whites, and tans, until the tones were just right. He inked three-dimensional nipple tattoos, more real than the real thing. Melanie went home and posted photos of the tattoos on her breast cancer support group Facebook page.

More cancer survivors came to the shop, local women who had never been tattooed, who saw Melanie's photos online. Mindful of their modesty, Trey put them in smocks that revealed only the breast he was working on. He played their favorite music, ignoring Lester's complaint that he couldn't tattoo to eighties rock 'n' roll. Understanding what it meant to be disfigured, Trey opened the shop early and closed late to ink them. He corrected work done by other tattoo artists, nipples as gray as dishwater, as small as ticks, or shaped like apricots.

Trey's nipples, clients said, were more beautiful than the ones they had before cancer. They not only looked real, they felt real. Soft mounds, they grew hard under a lover's tongue. Trey basked in his clients' gratitude, never asking how such things were possible. "You saved my life," said one woman. "You performed a miracle," said another. At first Trey thought they were exaggerating, but after a while he believed them.

~~~~~~~~~~

"You're the Florence Nightingale of tattoo artists. But it's not art," Nava said, switching on her ultrasonic toothbrush.

"Just because it's functional? Maybe it's folk art." He had to speak up to be heard above the brush. "You don't mind, do you?"

She shut the machine. "Mind what?"

"Me doing nipples."

"They're not real nipples."

He wanted to object.

Nava applied anti-wrinkle cream around her eyes. Trey trimmed the hair on his forearm, so the nude—his first and only tattoo—would stand out.

~~~~~~~~~~

Alisande sat on the edge of the barber chair, sketching. "It's like a hospital in here. It's a weird vibe. With your following, you could open your own shop, a medical tattoo shop."

On the couch, Trey sat, gripping his knees. He missed tattooing nudes, which were as close as his new art had come to his paintings. "I don't want to do only medical tattoos."

She looked up. "That's all you *are* doing. It's spooking our other customers."

"Are you firing me?"

"I'm not firing you. I'm suggesting you open your own place. Our numbers are way down. Not yours. Yours are fine. Mine and Lester's. The shop's." She showed him the image she had drawn. It was a tombstone with the inscription *RIP Mountain Ink.*

On Trey's last day, Alisande gave him a cap with the name of his new shop, Fine, and threw a party for him. All of his clients had been invited. The medical clients admired his older tattoos: nudes and skeletons and scripted words of inspiration and loss. After a few shots of tequila, they showed off their nipples to applause.

The new establishment thrived. Trey raised his prices. His fees were nothing compared to what doctors demanded. Symbols of health—a snake entwined around Asclepius's rod, the Tao, and lotus flowers—adorned the walls. Knowing his clients' immune systems were weak, Trey took extra precautions, wearing a surgical gown and mask, scrubbing often. The shop smelled like antiseptic.

Trey began to earn as much as Nava, and for the first time in their married life he didn't have to ask for money. One evening, Nava came looking for him. He was lying on their bed, watching PBS's *NewsHour.*

"There was a stack of bills on the dining-room table," she said.

"I paid them." He waited for her to thank him.

She massaged her neck like she did when she had a muscle spasm. "Why?"

"Because for once I could."

"Where are they?"

He was beginning to get annoyed. "I mailed them."

She watched the talking heads on TV debate a point. "Did you remember to put stamps on the envelopes?"

"Nava."

"Fine. Next time tell me so I won't think I misplaced them."

~~~~~~~~~

At a cocktail party, Trey overheard Nava tell a colleague her husband was an artist. She asked a bartender to refill her Merlot and mentioned a gallery that carried Trey's paintings, though they hadn't offered his work for years. Trey finished his Scotch and ordered another.

That night, as Nava slipped out of her bra, Trey bent toward her and said, "Perhaps a little more brown."

"What?"

"Nothing." Embarrassed, he turned away.

She covered her breasts with her arms. "Were you critiquing my nipples?"

"I wouldn't do that."

She put on her nightgown in the bathroom.

Browsing Internet porn the next day, Trey rolled his mouse over a nipple and enlarged it. He wasn't aroused. The color struck him as too pink. He wanted to get in there with his own colors, make a correction. Just because the breast was real didn't mean it couldn't be improved.

At the shop, he began tattooing healthy women. He enlarged areolas and darkened nipples. Some women brought photographs of breasts, images torn from magazines for Trey to use as models. Others left it up to him. He was the artist, after all.

A client returned to the shop accompanied by her husband, a skeletal man whose shoulders curved inward. "What can you do for *him*?" she asked.

Trey knew how light reflected off of the human body. His understanding of anatomy was as intimate as a surgeon's. Using three-dimensional tattoos that relied on contrast and shadow, Trey added a six-pack to the man's abdomen, biceps and triceps to his arms. When the client put his shirt back on, the buttons gapped.

Filling in another man's receding hairline, Trey matched the shade exactly. As the customer stepped from the shop, his bangs ruffled in the wind. Trey narrowed a woman's ankles and enlarged her eyes. Although he had once admired his subjects' imperfections, now he imagined correcting all their flaws.

Standing at the kitchen counter, Nava mashed an avocado, while Trey filled a ceramic bowl with chips. "You're so quick to change all these people," Nava said. "But I don't see you getting any so-called improvements."

Trey's chin dropped to his chest. "I can't tattoo myself. If I could, do you think I would still look like this?"

The next day, though, he closed the shop early and lined up inks, caps, and needles before a full-length mirror. He shaved, washed his face and body with green soap, and wiped himself with alcohol. He began by minimizing the flesh around his eyes and erasing his moles. Slowly he worked his way down his body. As the hours passed, his back started to ache and his fingers cramped, grasping the machine, but he continued, correcting the smallest imperfections. When he finished, his skin was tan. His neck and ears appeared perfectly proportioned. He was wrinkleless and muscular. Though tattoos normally take weeks to heal, the ones Trey inked healed as soon as the needle was lifted. Trey rushed home to show Nava.

Seeing a stranger enter her bedroom, Nava screamed, and she didn't stop screaming until she heard Trey's nasal voice. She demanded he undress and examined him up close and from the opposite end of the room.

"Don't you like it?"

"I married you, not Superman," she said, running her nails over his pecs.

Later, as they lay tangled and short of breath, he asked, "You're not even tempted?"

"You seem to find me attractive the way I am."

"Touché," he said, and disappeared again between her perfect imperfect thighs.

Grasping the coffeepot the next morning, Nava stared at him, forgetting to pour.

"Everything okay?" Trey said, holding out his cup.

"Keep talking," she said. "So I know it's you."

~~~~~~~~

Trey wasn't accustomed to being attractive. He startled the first time a stranger smiled at him. It must be someone from the shop, he thought, a client or the bookkeeper, but it wasn't anyone he knew, just someone moved by the gentleness of his eyes and the perfect slope of his forehead. He didn't know what to say when his massage therapist refused to charge him. "Just tell people I worked on you," she said, as she kneaded muscles he only appeared to have. It was strange and pleasant to be welcome wherever he went.

At Fine, he installed additional chairs and hung three-way mirrors. When space opened up next door, Trey expanded. He trained apprentices, who became first-rate tattoo artists but couldn't remake a client the way Trey could. While customers waited, cashiers explained installment and family plans and served espresso and chai.

A framed copy of *Buzzfeed*'s write-up of the shop, featuring his picture and the headline, "Where Beauty Is Made," hung behind the counter, and he never got tired of looking at it. Nava had taken it down from their bedroom wall. "Put it in the scrapbook with the others," she said. "I know what you look like."

One Saturday, he found her poring over their wedding album.

"We should redo those," he said.

"Never."

"In Chicago. You could wear your dress."

"You can't rewrite history."

He thought he could. He pictured her with a waist as thin as a reed, a behind like a firm plum. But when he mentioned it to her a week later, she scowled and refused to look at the sketches he held out.

~~~~~~~~

As Trey was reviewing receipts one afternoon, Melanie pushed open the door to the shop. She raked her fingers through cropped hair. "I relapsed!" The doctors' poisons weren't working anymore, she said. Maybe there was something Trey could do?

Trey didn't know what to say. He hated to tell her no. Maybe he could do it. It seemed natural after all he had done. What an accomplishment it would be! Melanie would live to play with grandchildren, undisturbed by illness. He rose light-headed from his seat. He looked around. Energy—and what was life if not energy?—pulsed through the tattoo machines. Artists bent over clients, blessing them with line and shade. He was glad Melanie had come to him.

He led her to the back, telling the others he didn't want to be disturbed. While he lit incense and queued up Bach choral music, she undressed and lay naked on the table, goose pimples peppering her pale skin, her arms and legs limp, hope and terror competing for her expression. He mixed dozens of colors, ones that had never been in the shop before and he hadn't ordered, and others that were his staples. Unmindful of dwindling daylight and the silence that fell over the front of the shop, he took his time. He tattooed perfectly proportioned, radiant breasts, robust and healthy, as full of life as wailing newborn twins. He sensed an immediate improvement in his client.

When Melanie saw the breasts, she wept and kissed his cheeks. "You saved my life."

She was halfway out the door when he shouted, "You should probably keep seeing your doctor." He wasn't sure if she heard.

He took Nava out to dinner that night. The hostess of the five-star restaurant embraced him and led them to his regular table by the window. Above him hung mounted elk and bull moose; before him lay gilt-edged china on linen cloths.

A diner stopped by their table, holding out a cocktail napkin and a pen. "Doc, make it out, 'To Gerald, my best work,'" he said.

Raising her eyebrows, Nava mouthed the word *Doc*. Trey ignored her.

"What's the occasion?" she asked when they were finally alone.

As he adjusted his cuff links, he said: "I think I might have saved a patient's life today."

She choked on her water. When she was able to talk, she asked, "How did you manage that?"

He told her about Melanie and she stared at him, speechless.

"It's possible," he said.

Nava shook her head. "She should have gone to see her doctor."

~~~~~~~~~~~~

Melanie died three weeks later. When Trey heard, he slipped into bed and stayed there. All he could think about was the day he had met her and tattooed her arm in celebration. He wondered what would become of her daughter, Grace.

A week went by. "You need a shower," Nava said, opening windows.

Trey rolled onto his side, facing the wall. He still could not stop thinking of Melanie, how he had taken her to the back of the shop and all but promised her life.

"Did you really think you could cure her?"

He didn't answer.

"You're not a doctor. You're a tattoo artist." She insisted he sit in an armchair while she changed the bedding. Then she handed him fresh pajamas. "I recommend washing before you put these on."

He discarded his dirty pajamas on the floor but didn't shower before returning to bed naked.

The next day, he called Melanie's husband to offer condolences and learned Melanie had stopped treatment after seeing him. Trey couldn't shut out the image of Melanie's face, looking to him for hope. When he tried to get out of bed, he could hardly move, feeling feverish, his muscles aching.

"You helped her feel better while she was alive. That's something," Nava said that night, pulling off her pumps.

"Now you're a fan."

Nava ordered dinners from his favorite restaurants, setting them on a tray beside him, pea soup with ham one night, brisket another, roast chicken a third. The meats reminded him of Melanie's flesh, and he fasted.

She scheduled an appointment with a psychiatrist, but when the day arrived, Trey refused to get in the car. What would a psychiatrist tell him that he didn't already know? He had thought he was an angel of mercy, when in fact he was the angel of death.

Nava entreated an acupuncturist to make a house call. The woman arrived around eleven, knocked on the door, and finally phoned Trey's cell. He ignored her, because he didn't deserve to be healed.

~~~~~~~~

As she was leaving for work one day, Nava set a drawing pad and a mechanical pencil next to him on the wrinkled sheets. "I don't know what else to do," she muttered.

When she was gone, he snatched them. He couldn't help himself. He sat up and arranged a pillow behind his back. Without thinking, he sketched nudes, anchors, cobras, nipples, his hand moving for hours, never pausing except to turn the page, until the pad was full.

He dressed and hurried to his studio in the barn, finding windows coated with dust and his easel toppled. He tore open boxes of paints and brushes, righted the easel, and stretched canvases. From memory, he painted Melanie, first with nipples, then without, and finally just her face, eyes hungry for life and a soft mouth. As he worked, he heard Nava's car come up the driveway. Though the light in the studio was on, she didn't come in, and he didn't go out.

At a medical center that had sent him women wanting nipples, he invited cancer patients to have their portraits done. Male and female, young and old, ambulatory and in wheelchairs, he painted them. Word spread in chemo-infusion rooms and hospital lobbies across Denver and in Cheyenne, and the sick found him. He captured them as they were, however bald or ashen, with sunken, grieving eyes or gazes full and hopeful. He changed nothing.

Why his subjects wished to be painted, he didn't know, and he didn't ask. It was enough that they came. Many died before their portraits were completed.

Canvases multiplied in his studio, leaning against walls, drying on tables, hanging from the ceiling. He gave the work to his subjects or to their families if they wanted it. He hung portraits at Fine, though clients and staff complained, and business dropped off. He rented a giant storage locker for the rest.

Over time, Trey's body forgot the changes he had made. The flesh around his eyes thickened, and his skin paled. A series of enormous moles, like a mountain chain, erupted on his nose and cheeks one day. He considered tattooing himself again but decided against it. Though tattoos had made him look better, he didn't like what he'd become. He worried how Nava would feel. Perhaps she'd grown accustomed to his improved appearance. When she entered the studio that night, he turned to hide his face. "I'm sorry," he said.

She studied him from the doorway and then came close, stroking his cheek. "For what?" He was working on a painting of a woman on a tattooing table, scars where her breasts should have been, an angel on her arm. The woman's eyes were closed. Her flesh was tinged with blue. "She's beautiful," Nava said.

"It took me forever to ink that angel. I barely knew what I was doing. She was very patient."

"She had no reason to be in a hurry then."

It was the best work he had ever done, and it would end up in the storage locker where the dead gathered, talking perhaps of failed treatments, useless vanities, a mythical tattoo artist who could cure cancer. He couldn't say for sure, because each time he rolled up the door to add another to their number, they quieted, and all he heard was the rattle of metal and the faint vibration of a tattoo machine.

The Infidelity of Judah Maccabee

At forty-two, Barry Waxman no longer had to wonder why everyone he knew had gotten theirs while he was still waiting for his. His life was full. At the Great Northeastern Insurance Company, he managed a dozen actuaries in white button-down shirts. He lived with Anette, a thin woman with a Nordic nose and long fingers that were always moving, bettering his life—filleting fish, unclogging drains, debugging his computer. His cat, Mac, was short haired and gray. Vertical pupils cut his yellow eyes, black slits that emptied into an endless universe. If he wasn't massaging Barry's thighs with his thick paws, he was nipping the fleshy edge of Barry's palm or sandpapering it with his tongue.

Barry was content until looking out the window of his Brooklyn apartment one night he saw lights strung around streetlamps and a man wearing an elf hat. While he was at work the next day, Anette had a spruce tree delivered. In the three years they'd lived together, she had never done that before. She bolted the tree to a metal base, strung popcorn and tinsel, presenting him when he came home with a fait accompli: a six-foot-tall Christmas tree that dwarfed the electric menorah he had rested on the windowsill.

Christmas confirmed Barry's fear that as a Jew he would always be an outsider in America. Growing up, he had watched with envy while his schoolmates scribbled lists of presents, their anticipation growing as the holiday approached. But when Barry mentioned Christmas, his father exploded: "An excuse for pogroms!" Then he told Barry for the hundredth time about Cossacks who had bloodied his grandfather in Ukraine and cut off his beard. One after another, the homes on Barry's block lit up, while his remained stubbornly dark except for a small, flickering menorah, proof to his neighbors, Barry worried, that his family didn't belong.

As an adult, Barry resented that Christmas overshadowed Hanukkah. Menorahs and dreidels appeared as mere afterthoughts in shops, on single shelves or in dim corners, while Christmas hijacked entire establishments and his favorite eighties rock 'n' roll station, making it impossible for him to buy a pair of socks without considering the miracle of the birth of Jesus. The holiday intruded at Barry's job, too, where he was expected to play Secret Santa to a woman in human resources who consistently got his 401K contributions wrong. Perhaps, he thought, he should get her a calculator.

Anette hovered to one side of the tree. "Do you like it?" There was a tremor in her voice. He had expressed to her his reservations about the holiday. "I thought it would balance things out," she said.

He pressed his index finger to a ripe needle, relishing the sharp pain. "We've never had a tree," he said, as if his objection were based on the details of their short life together rather than the annals of his people.

"I always had one."

Mac sniffed the metal base of the tree, rubbed his back against it, and purred. "Mac likes it," Anette said.

Barry picked up the cat and showed him the menorah. "We're Jewish, Mac. Got it?" But when he set Mac down, the cat darted back to the tree.

The tree's fragrance was out of place in his apartment, and Barry had the odd sensation he had wandered into someone else's home. "How can I celebrate Christmas? Christians were responsible for the Crusades and the Inquisition. The Church prevents people from using birth control and oppresses gays."

Anette tore a strip of gold tinsel from the tree, and it floated to the floor. Mac batted it back and forth, then reared up on his hind legs before pouncing on it. "Is that how you think of me?" Anette said. "As a gay oppressor?"

"Not you."

"Other Christians."

"Right."

"Do you see how prejudiced that is? My parents weren't responsible for the Crusades or the Inquisition. And homosexuals are welcome in their congregation."

Barry lifted Mac into his arms and sat at the dining-room table, keeping the cat from the tree. "Your parents served ham when we visited them because their German butcher assured them a rabbi blessed it."

"You like ham."

"They didn't know that."

"You asked for seconds."

"I was being polite." The cat wriggled until Barry released

him. Picking gray fur off his black wool pants, Barry said, "You ambushed me."

Anette sank into a chair next to him and stuffed a leftover roll of tinsel into a department store bag. "I knew if I asked, you'd say no. But it hardly seems fair for my ornaments to gather dust in the closet, while you light your menorah."

"You never said anything."

"I kept waiting for you to ask. Whether I missed having a tree."

Barry approached the spruce again and fingered the ornaments he could tell she had hung for him, the silver Stars of David, the dreidels, and the latkes that resembled plastic barf people bought as gag gifts. He sighed. "Where'd you find all these?"

"At the Jews for Jesus store in Cadman Plaza."

Curled at the base of the tree, Mac slept.

~~~~~~~~~

The next night was the first night of Hanukkah. Barry left work early and stopped at Gristedes to pick up latkes and applesauce. Not as good as the ones his mother had made from a Manischewitz mix, the latkes nevertheless buttressed his soul against candy canes and fruitcakes. Next to the cash register, buried at the bottom of a stack of holiday CDs, below Bing Crosby's *White Christmas* and James Brown's *Funky Christmas*, he found a klezmer CD and on impulse he bought that, too. Cat treats shaped like dreidels filled a bowl. He grabbed a handful for Mac and pictured the cat eating one and cleaning his whiskers.

It was his tenth Hanukkah with Mac, a decade since he had come upon a young girl tending a litter of kittens in a torn cardboard box a few blocks from his apartment. The girl sat on a concrete stoop next to the box. "We can't keep them." She shoved down the flaps to give Barry a better view. "Cats don't care if you give away their kittens."

Three black kittens tumbled over one another and a tiny gray shivered in a corner, head pressed to the cardboard. Barry was returning from the supermarket, a heavy bag of groceries digging into each hand. Mustard-colored high-rises loomed over the Brooklyn street. Through the window of every apartment, Barry thought he saw a Christmas tree, sparkling red and green. A giant wreath clung to every door. He dreaded returning to his empty apartment, to his simple electric menorah, no one to give him a gift and no one to receive one from him. The kittens chirped like baby birds.

"Maybe you want two," the girl said, shoulder-length brown hair slipping from a ponytail someone had halfheartedly banded. Her pea coat, unbuttoned, flapped in wind that bustled down the hi-rise canyon.

Consolidating his shopping bags in one hand, Barry scooped the gray kitten in his palm. Light and delicate as an egg, its fragility moved him. He cocooned it in the pocket of his black wool overcoat.

"I think he's hungry," the girl said, stamping her feet to warm them. Her worn jeans fell short of her ankles.

He rummaged through his bags and found a box of butter cookies. As he handed it to her, her mouth fell open and he noticed how thin she was, moon shadows falling on the inward curve of her cheeks. While she tore open the box, he set his other bags next to her and continued home.

Back at his apartment with the kitten, he switched on the menorah. He sang holiday songs from his childhood—"Oh Hanukkah" and "I Have a Little Dreidel"—and danced with the animal pressed to his chest. They shared a dust-covered can of sardines. The oily fish had never tasted so good. He named the cat Judah Maccabee, after the warrior-priest who led the Jews to victory over the Hellenists, and called him Mac for short.

Why had he not always had a cat? His father had thought animals were dirty, to be kept outside if at all. But Barry found in Mac a companion superior in many respects to his human associates. Irritations and slights—the disappearance of *Insurance Science History and Practice* from his office, not being invited when other actuaries went to lunch—faded when he stroked Mac's velvet coat. He forgot he was the only one of four siblings still unmarried, that his best friend, Gregory, had stopped returning his calls after taking up with a pale, plump woman named Basha. The cat required little in the way of entertainment. A string of dental floss drawn across the couch could occupy him for hours. He batted a plush mouse across the floor and talked—how he talked! A machinelike purr, a high cry of hunger, a sharp protest when Barry accidentally stepped on him.

As Barry rode the subway home from Gristedes to Anette and Mac, he pictured his electric menorah glowing in the third-story window. Maybe next year he would light an oil menorah. He had always been afraid of the mess, and he knew the actuarial risk of lighting any kind of fire at home. The whole place could burn down if you weren't careful. The Gristedes bag jounced on his lap with the motion of the train, releasing the smell of fried potato pancakes into the subway car, forecasting an evening during which his small family would celebrate Hanukkah.

In the hall outside his apartment, he reached for his key and

heard "I Saw Mommy Kissing Santa Claus." He imagined it playing in the apartment of a neighbor, perhaps Cindy Johnson, who
clomped about in wedge heels, a silver cross nestled in her cleavage—
not that he looked.

Barry had tried to forget the tree, but when he opened the door
there it was, crowding his dining room. As it turned out, the music
was coming from the radio in his kitchen. Anette sang along as she
slid a tray of pastel-colored Christmas cookies into the oven. She had
placed the mixing bowl on the floor, and Mac was licking the pink
batter. On a rack, a second tray of cookies cooled. Her holiday was
taking over every room in the house.

"Do you have to do that now? It's the first night of Hanukkah,"
he shouted over the chorus. Stainless-steel cookie cutters littered the
kitchen table.

"I'll just set the timer on these and we'll turn on the menorah."
She removed her apron, which had reindeer flying across it.

He snapped off the radio, but it was too late. His evening was
spoiled. Why couldn't his home be Jewish for one night? His future
would consist of baked hams and presents wrapped in mistletoe
paper. Next she would want to celebrate Easter.

The kitchen smelled like someone else's childhood. Barry's mouth
watered, and he wondered if that was how assimilation began, with
baked goods. He worried he was betraying the memories of his father
and grandfather. When he offered Mac a dreidel treat, the cat sniffed
it and went back to the bowl of batter.

~~~~~~~~~~

Four thirty the next morning, Mac failed to bat Barry on the nose.
Barry had always complained about Mac waking him so early to be

fed, but it was a loving complaint. He would set a plate of kibble in the corner of the bedroom and close his eyes, the sound of the cat crunching like a white noise machine lulling him back to sleep.

When he woke to his alarm at six, his first thought was something terrible had happened to Mac. He toed the gray lump asleep at his feet and elicited a bitter cry that reassured him. Perhaps, he reasoned, Mac simply had not been hungry. Out of curiosity, he checked Mac's bowl and found it had been filled with kibble in the night, half of which had been consumed.

"Honey," he said, shaking Anette. "Did you feed Mac?"

She was snoring, sucking long strands of delicate blond hair into her mouth and then exhaling them. He shook her again.

"Barry, I'm sleeping," she groaned, her eyes still closed.

"Did you feed Mac?"

"Yes."

"Why?" It was less a question than a protest.

"Because he was hungry."

"How did you know?"

"He tapped my nose."

~~~~~~~~~~

The remains of Barry's lunch—wax paper dotted with mustard and an empty Sprite can—lay on his desk. Slumped in his chair, Barry imagined Mac tapping Anette's nose and Anette smiling coquettishly before opening her eyes. The relish he had eaten was giving him heartburn. He tried to tell himself it didn't matter who fed the cat, to reassure himself his bond with Mac was indestructible, but then he pictured Mac reaching for Anette.

He phoned his older sister Gladys, who had four children and a way of analyzing his problems that soothed him. When she talked, he could almost hear his mother explaining why he was better off being excluded when neighborhood boys flipped baseball cards or played pickup basketball. "They probably have lice—or worse, worms." He missed his mother.

"It's nothing," Gladys said. "The cat didn't want to bother you. He knows you need your sleep to be sharp for work."

"He likes her because she's blond and her fingers always smell like fish," Barry said. He was looking up Anette's life expectancy.

"Whose side of the bed does he sleep on?"

"Mine."

"Then you have nothing to worry about."

He made a note to give Gladys a discount when she renewed her policies.

Gray light filtering into his bedroom woke Barry the next morning. The cat had already eaten. He wanted to instruct Anette not to feed Mac, to remind her Mac was his cat, but he despised his own insecurity. Of course there was no talking to the cat.

He remembered how peaceful their lives had been before Anette. He would stretch out on the couch with a James Patterson thriller, Mac swatting the pages as he turned them. They would eat dinner together, Mac out of his bowl, and Barry straight from a Swanson's microwavable package. There had been no alien holidays to endure.

After dinner that night, the cat climbed into Anette's lap rather than his, purring as loud as a jackhammer when Anette massaged his neck. It was the third night of Hanukkah, and the lights on the menorah jerked and twitched. Mac kneaded *her* thigh, nipped *her* hand, and rolled onto his side, inviting Anette to scratch his belly— something he had never allowed Barry to do. They pleasured each other right in front of him, without shame. Barry fled to the bedroom.

When his jealousy subsided, he remembered he owed his relationship with Anette to Mac. Gladys had sent him a link to an online dating site, but Barry hesitated to click on it. Women, he believed, were not attracted to pale actuaries. Tan investment bankers, yes. Ruddy lawyers, certainly. But not men like him. From Barry's lap, Mac pawed the computer, bringing up the profile of a blue-eyed accountant—a CPA no less—staring impatiently back at Barry. Like him, Anette had never been married and had spent her life devoted to numbers. Her skin was translucent. A soul mate? Barry had dismissed such unquantifiable notions in the past, but now he let himself imagine a perfect pairing, created in heaven even before he was born. As quickly as he could, he composed a profile and showed it to Mac before posting it.

On their first date, they chatted about standard deviations and probability distributions. They ate dim sum and joked about the odds of both having scientific calculator keychains. When she laughed, she revealed horsey gap teeth, and he immediately wanted to knock his own teeth against them. On their third date, he made love to her in his apartment, under freshly laundered sheets and a quilt embedded with cat fur. He probed her teeth with his tongue and walked his hands over her knobby frame, learning the motions that pleased her.

When he attended the symphony with Anette, Barry heard a richness in the sound that was new. Watching a romantic comedy with her, he imagined himself the leading man and Anette the leading woman, her smile as bright as Jennifer Aniston's. She would pat him lightly on the hand before pointing out something in the Sunday paper they shared, and slip her arm through his as they walked to a diner for brunch, her touch making him feel, at long last, that he was fully participating in life.

At first Anette and Mac ignored each other. Mac avoided her feet and turned away from dental floss she accidentally dropped. Barry had to correct Anette when she used the pronoun *it* to refer to Mac. He worried they weren't getting along. After she moved in and made fish stew—adding butter and onion and chunk after chunk of haddock—Mac warmed to her, rubbing against her ankles, head butting her belly when he found her in bed. Anette began to refer to him fondly as Big Mac.

~~~~~~~~~~

"Everything all right, Barry?" his boss asked the next day, when he was late turning in an end-of-year report. The woman was his age, pearls dotting her large earlobes, lines on her brow that darkened when she was annoyed.

"Formatting it right now," he said evenly. Brooding over holidays and cats, he had been distracted from his work. He wondered: *Why is the firm closed on Christmas but open on Hanukkah? I ought to sue.*

"Can I help?" his secretary whispered after his boss was gone.

"You can stay at your desk until I call you," he barked, though in the past they had always gotten along. He hadn't minded when she left early for her daughter's soccer games, and she had advised him on gifts for Anette.

A woman in black orthopedic shoes, clutching a maple cane, lurched onto the subway while he was riding home, but he pretended not to see. He had risen for her before, but now he reasoned, her ride was short, and he was not so young himself.

At home, as Barry put away his briefcase and took off his suit jacket, Mac followed him through the apartment crying. He picked the cat up and regarded him at arm's length. "This morning you wanted her, but now you'll settle for me." He harnessed the cat for a walk.

"Don't you want me to come?" Anette asked.

Wrapping a scarf around his neck, he avoided her eyes. "Maybe better if you didn't."

Mac pulled him through a park, under naked ash trees, the ground alongside the concrete path frozen. Yellow bulbs flickered behind filmy lampposts. The cat sniffed a Chihuahua in a pink sweater and licked the ears of a long-haired dachshund. He rubbed against a woman's stocking-clad legs, and she bent to pet him. Barry had once delighted in strangers' enjoyment of Mac, but now he imagined them stealing the cat's affection, and he headed home.

Anette had switched on the menorah—it was the fourth night of Hanukkah—and put on the klezmer CD. To his surprise, Barry discovered he didn't like klezmer, but grateful for the effort Anette was making, he threw up his hands and pretended to conduct the band.

For dinner Anette served warm, creamy blintzes with sour cream and applesauce. Barry sat back and admired the golden crepes. "Like the kind my mother used to buy," he said. He filled Anette's glass with seltzer and refilled it again when it was only half empty.

After they ate, Anette pulled Barry to her and they danced around the dining room, spinning away from the Christmas tree and back, the sounds of the fiddle and flute uplifting them. For once, his angular limbs moved gracefully, and though he was leading, he knew she was subtly guiding him.

When they tired, they sat on the floor, and Barry taught Anette how to spin the dreidel and the meaning of the Hebrew letters painted on its sides.

"Now I'm an honorary Jew," Anette said.

She'd be back to her tree tomorrow, Barry thought, but there was no harm in pretending for a night. Anette stripped foil from a chocolate coin, fed it to Barry, and licked her fingers.

Mac pounced on the dreidel and it skittered under the tree. Crawling after it, Barry was surrounded by a thick, living smell. It reminded him of the Catskill Mountains, where his family had rented a cabin for two weeks every summer when he was a child. His father traded a three-piece suit for swimming trunks, exposing anemic legs. His mother squeezed her head into a white rubber cap and dog-paddled in a small section of the lake cordoned off with plastic ropes and buoys. At a restaurant in town, his father ordered a cheeseburger, though at home they didn't mix milk and meat. "We're on vacation," his father said, when he saw Barry staring, and Barry ordered a milkshake to go with his lamb chops.

~~~~~~~~~~

"Forget Christmas, everyone loves cookies," Anette said in the morning, as she prepared a plate for Barry to take to work. Feeling like a traitor to his people, he set her homemade cookies—stars and trees, painted with icing and dotted with sprinkles—in the break room, a note, *from Barry and Anette*, alongside. Colleagues who had ignored him in the past stopped by his office. They asked about his holiday plans and shared company gossip. One pounded him on the back while wishing him Merry Christmas. Barry enjoyed the attention, blushing during the boisterous visit, but he resented it took Christmas to bring it about.

Christmas Eve fell on the seventh night of Hanukkah. Barry lit the menorah and Anette tuned the radio to a station playing carols. She poured eggnog and champagne, made roast duck with latkes on the side, the savory smells filling the apartment, torturing Mac, who paced in front of the oven while the duck cooked. Barry wondered why his holiday rated only a side dish.

Anette's family had always opened gifts on Christmas Eve. Barry gave her an antique slide rule for Hanukkah and for Christmas, tickets to the New York Philharmonic performing Handel's *Messiah*. For Mac, he bought a New York Mets collar and a pot of catnip. Anette plucked Barry's present from under the tree and handed it to him. Tearing away the tissue paper, he uncovered a photo of Anette and Mac in a heart-shaped frame, the cat curled in her lap, eyes half closed. "All your loves," Anette cooed, admiring the photo over his shoulder.

Barry stared at the picture. "It's like I don't even exist."

"Come on. It's to show how much we love you, me and Mac."

"Who took the picture?"

"We went to a studio."

"You took a family photo without me?" The picture frame slipped from Barry's fingers, and the glass broke as it hit the floor.

Mac hid under the couch. Anette knelt to gather the pieces of the broken gift.

"I need some air." Grabbing his coat, Barry left the apartment. Outside, he trudged down frigid, empty streets. Through brightly lit windows he saw rooms full of people celebrating.

Reviewing his relationship with Anette, Barry found slights everywhere. For his birthday, she had bought him an Italian sport coat and a pair of Hugo Boss loafers. Although grateful at the time, Barry now concluded she was ashamed of the way he dressed. When she introduced him to her parents, she said he was from Brooklyn and his ancestors had emigrated from Eastern Europe. Barry had to add he was Jewish. Was she ever planning to tell them? They were from Scandinavia, the mother six inches taller than Barry. Why had he ever thought it could work?

Hunger eventually drove him home. Anette had swept up the glass. No evidence of the photo remained. They sat at the dining-room table silently eating a cold meal.

Christmas Day, Barry studied loss models at the kitchen table, while in the living room, Anette caught up on new IRS regulations. Mac padded between the two, gnawing Anette's shoelaces, swatting the cuffs of Barry's pants. When Anette came into the kitchen to heat the kettle, Barry didn't look up from his laptop. He declined her offer of a cup of tea.

Darkness swept through the apartment. Though it was the last night of Hanukkah, Barry didn't bother to light the menorah. Anette hadn't cooked. They ate reheated leftovers while watching the evening news.

"Why don't we take Mac for a walk," Anette said after dinner.

"What else have we got to do?" Barry said, rinsing plates and stacking them in the dishwasher.

Barry harnessed the cat and they walked along the sidewalk, talking only of mundane things, when they had to be back at work and their need to buy coffee and eggs. As they passed the apartment building where Barry had found Mac so many years before, he glanced through a window into a lobby with a giant Christmas tree and paused when he saw a girl in her late teens, gathering with her family to go out for the holiday. The girl's down coat hung open over a thick wool sweater and pressed pants. Her hair, neatly brushed, shone.

"Do you know her?" Anette asked.

"She could be the girl who gave me Mac. She's about the right age. But it was a long time ago." Barry remembered how fragile Mac had seemed; how worried he had been the kitten would suffocate in his pocket, the only place he knew to keep Mac warm; how relieved he had been to get home and find the kitten still alive.

Anette smiled, her teeth enormous in the streetlamp glow. "Our Mac." She linked her arm with Barry's, and he reluctantly left it there.

Mac jerked the leash forward, pulling Barry and Anette along. Clouds obscured the moon and threatened snow. Shivering, Barry tightened his scarf. It wasn't long before they arrived at a street he didn't recognize, without lampposts, stores shuttered and exotic lettering on signs.

"Did you mean to go this way?" Anette asked.

"It's him," Barry said, motioning with his chin toward Mac. Barry tripped over a raised curbstone as he struggled to keep up. Glancing around, he tried to get his bearings but couldn't. "Who knows what he's after?"

"He must smell a female in heat." Anette laughed and squeezed Barry's arm.

Barry didn't see anything funny about another box of helpless kittens, and Mac the father. But what could he do? He lowered his head into the wind. Tethered to Mac, his landscape would constantly change, the cat moving faster, always, than Barry wanted to go.

No Shortage of Birds

〰〰〰〰〰〰
〰〰〰

A month after Charlotte's father died, her mother brought home a parakeet. "You can play with him after school," she said, as if Charlotte were a small child who needed someone to plan her activities.

Charlotte was in junior high. "I don't want it," she said. "Take it back." It would take more than a bird to make Charlotte forget she hadn't saved her father.

Her mother set the cage on the dining-room table and spread paper towels over the plastic bottom. The table sat six, four more than they needed. "Picture him riding on your shoulder. Wouldn't that be nice?"

The bird stared with black, unfeeling eyes. Its belly was the pastel blue of a Popsicle. Charlotte's mother stuck a pumpkin seed through the bars, and the bird snatched it with its sharp, yellow beak. "See how friendly he is? What do you want to call him?"

"I'm not calling it anything."

"How about Mellie, in honor of Dad." Her mother hadn't spoken her father's nickname since he died.

"You want to give Dad's name to a *bird*?" The parakeet, which had been investigating the cage, froze. "Dad hated birds!"

"Keep your voice down. You're scaring him." She slipped another pumpkin seed through the bars. "Besides, your father didn't hate birds. He was allergic to them."

Mail fell through the front-door slot. Charlotte went after it, relieved to escape her mother, who had been pale and distracted since her father died but was now smiling over the bird in a way that made Charlotte uneasy.

Condolence cards still arrived on most days, addressed to her mother, Elisha Melott; to the Melott Family; and even occasionally to Charlotte. Her social studies teacher had made the entire class write them before Charlotte returned to school.

There were no cards for Charlotte today. She hoped she never saw another—such useless expressions of sympathy, with childish drawings of flowers or the sun. The new issue of *Golf Magazine* appeared among catalogs and bills, her father's name, Corbin Melott, on the mailing label. Charlotte dropped the rest of the mail onto the floor and took the magazine to her room.

She opened it at her desk. Pictures of pros like her father filled every page, men and women lining up shots, driving balls, pushing tees into the earth. Charlotte searched for an image of her father. She found ads for the putter he used, his brands of balls, bags, and gloves, the caps and shoes he wore. But she didn't see him. In the back of the magazine, his name appeared in the standings. He was ranked ninety-seventh in the world. She tore out the page and fastened it to her corkboard, covering an image of Lydia Ko waving a trophy at the Kia Classic. She threw the rest of the magazine away, thinking how unfair it was for golfers ranked below her dad to move up through no effort of their own.

They had been at the Raven Golf Course in Phoenix. Every Sunday he wasn't on the tour, she and her father played. He had hit a long drive and was watching it sail down the fairway. At the same time, an errant shot hooked toward him. Charlotte saw the ball coming, as surprising as a comet, but her father didn't. She refused to believe it would hit him. The day was too perfect, sun providing gentle March warmth and lighting up the grass, her father beside her, whistling in appreciation of his shot as he leaned against his driver. He wore a Callaway cap set back, smashing wiry curls. The ball sped toward him, but she was too shocked to cry out. It struck his temple with a muffled thud, a sound she would always remember as being too small for the damage it did, and he collapsed at her feet. Only then did she manage to speak. "Dad?" She knelt beside him, her hands tugging his arm. But there was no answer.

The party behind them drove up in a cart. Charlotte touched her father's cheek. Above it rose a bump larger than the ball itself, straining against his skin. "Dad?"

Paramedics moved her aside and took her father. Someone must have called. A golfer who knew him drove her to the hospital and waited with her until her mother arrived.

While surgeons worked on her father, she and her mother sat in a windowless room on vinyl furniture, a CNN anchor broadcasting in what might as well have been a foreign language. They ignored the hot water dispenser and tea bags provided for their comfort. When they returned home late that night, her mother told her: His brain had swelled; he was in a coma.

~~~~~~~~~

They'd had the parakeet for two weeks. When Charlotte's mother wasn't at work, managing money for professional athletes, the bird perched on her shoulder or played with toys she had bought: bells, a beaded carousel, mirrored rings. "What would I do without you?" Elisha said, as she fed it almonds and pistachios. She scratched its neck, rubbed its belly, and called it "my little budgie."

At first Charlotte suspected her mother only pretended to like the bird—the way Elisha had once pretended to enjoy chard, to get Charlotte to eat it. If Charlotte approached, the bird backed up and beat its wings.

Preoccupied with the parakeet, Elisha seemed to forget Charlotte's father. She traded somber blouses for sparkly tops that attracted the bird. Each night she moved the cage from the den and set it next to her in bed before covering it. Charlotte could no longer deny her mother's affection for the bird was real. Some nights Charlotte missed her father so much *she* wanted to crawl in next to her mother, but she couldn't, not unless she wanted to share her father's side of the bed with the bird.

The year before he died, her father had earned more than a million dollars. To celebrate, the family went to a restaurant where waiters wore tuxedos. Her father traded his Acura for a Mercedes and bought her mother a diamond-encrusted pin shaped like a golf cart.

They surprised Charlotte with a new two-thousand-dollar bike for Christmas.

After her father died, Charlotte overheard her mother on the phone saying if they were careful, the insurance money would be enough. Charlotte wanted to know: careful about what? She couldn't ask without admitting she'd been eavesdropping. Maybe her mother would return Charlotte's bike. Or they'd have to move to a tiny apartment like the one where her cousins lived. She'd never be able to get away from the bird.

Elisha was always encouraging Charlotte to get to know Mellie. One afternoon, holding out the parakeet, Elisha said, "Come on, feel how soft he is."

Charlotte decided to give Mellie a chance. But as she reached out to stroke the bird, it screeched and bit her finger.

At the dining-room table the next night, her mother fed the parakeet banana slices from a plate while making kissing sounds. Bananas were Charlotte's favorite. She tightened a fist around the book report she had brought to show her mother. "Are there any more?" she asked.

"Sorry, last one," Elisha said. "How about a peach?"

Charlotte ran a finger around the edge of the plate, itching to fling it across the room. "You know I like bananas."

"I'll get more tomorrow."

"They won't be ripe."

"I'll get ripe ones."

"Those will be too ripe." She slapped the report on the table.

"There's plenty for both of you." Her mother offered her a slice on a fork. Exposed to air, the flesh had browned.

~~~~~~~~~~~~

The Arizona Diamondbacks were playing the Colorado Rockies. Charlotte and her mother sat on the couch in the den and watched the game.

"I love you," Elisha said to the parakeet, who had flown to the top of the TV and was walking along its edge.

"I love you," the bird squawked.

"I'm trying to watch," Charlotte said, furious to hear her mother offer the bird endearments that rightfully belonged to Charlotte and her father. The night before, Elisha had forgotten to say "I love you" to Charlotte after kissing her good night.

"It's just a beer ad."

"I like the commercials."

Her father's trophies lined up dull and abandoned on a glass shelf. Her mother hadn't bothered to dust or polish them even once. When the bird took off from the TV, it landed on his Barbasol Championship cup, but not before soiling the trophy next to it with a fat green dropping. Charlotte leaped from the couch and swatted the bird, catching its tail with the back of her hand and dislodging three feathers, the bird screaming, "I love you! I love you!"

Elisha came after Charlotte. She grabbed her by the arm and shook her. "He's a member of the family." Her mother had never touched her before with anything but kindness.

Later, as Charlotte undressed for bed, she examined her arm and found a bruise. Down the hall she heard her mother singing R.E.M.'s "Man on the Moon," the bird repeating the chorus. "We're made for each other," Elisha said to the parakeet.

In the weeks after the accident, Elisha had dragged Charlotte to see a psychiatrist. Charlotte wondered what Dr. Birnbaum would have had to say about the bird.

~~~~~~~~~~

Two months had passed since Charlotte's father died. Outside, the temperature soared to a hundred and five degrees. The company her mother had contacted to fix the air-conditioning hadn't shown up.

At three, her mother called to remind Charlotte to refill the bird's water. "He could die without it."

"Yeah, okay," Charlotte said.

"Do it now."

"I'm talking to you on the phone now."

"As soon as you hang up."

"Okay."

After the call, Charlotte lay in bed with her iPad and pulled up the Katy Perry channel on YouTube. Clicking *All*, she raised the sound as high as it would go and closed her eyes. Over and over she saw the ball hit her father. The music drowned out the sound but couldn't erase the image.

The desert sun baked the house. Sweat coated Charlotte's palms, and she wiped them on her denim cutoffs. When she rose to give the bird water at five, it was too late. In the den, the bird lay at the bottom of the cage, rigid white head and stiff blue belly, dark eyes open. She looked away, through a window that opened to their backyard. A sparrow nested in a palo verde tree, and crows perched on the wood fence. She told herself there was no shortage of birds, and with the parakeet gone maybe Elisha would go back to being her mother and would remember the real Mellie was dead and behave the way a widow should.

Charlotte poked her hand into the cage and petted the bird's soft feathers. She touched its smooth, tiny beak, feeling the sharp point. Lying utterly still, the bird couldn't help but remind her of her father. Taking a pink foot between finger and thumb, she said, "Good-bye, Mellie."

At the side of the house, the contents of the trash container fermented, filling the air with a sweet, rotten scent. A hot wind seared her face. "Too soon he was taken," she said, the words of the pastor at her father's funeral.

It was nothing to kill a bird when you had already killed your father. Opening the trash container, she uncinched a plastic bag and pressed the parakeet beneath banana peels, Styrofoam, coffee grounds, an empty milk carton, and other discarded layers of their lives. The plastic lid slapped shut.

Her mother would be upset. But it would serve her right for having tried to replace Charlotte's father with a bird. And what could Elisha do? Take away Charlotte's phone? The joke would be on her mother, because no one else called or texted Charlotte, and Charlotte had given up on social media. "You're too sad," her former best friend, Maxine, had explained before blocking her on Snapchat.

Back inside, Charlotte filled the bird's water bottle, so her mother wouldn't find it empty. She spread out her math homework on the dining-room table as if she were doing it. When she was younger, her father had helped her with math, drawing half and quarter pies with his fancy silver pen to teach her about fractions. Finishing a lesson, they would go into the kitchen and eat bakery pie, large cherry-apple slices, raining crumbs on the embroidered tablecloth and the tile floor. Her father used the same silver pen to write checks and sometimes handed it to her, trusting her to fill in the amount and to figure the new balance.

Lately, she had stopped doing her math homework. "Are you all right, Charlotte?" Mrs. Rapps asked when she didn't turn it in. Each day, "Are you all right?" Charlotte wanted to poke out the woman's soft gray eyes with her father's pen.

Charlotte usually greeted her mother with silence, but now, even before her mother had time to set down her briefcase, Charlotte hugged her, rubbing her cheek against her mother's shirt and breathing in her worn-out smell. *You still have me,* she wanted to say, anticipating her mother's grief at losing the bird. "I'm sorry," she said instead.

Her mother's thin, dark eyebrows came together. Charlotte thought it was ridiculous for Elisha to pluck them when there was no longer anyone to impress.

Elisha headed toward the den. For a moment the house was quiet. Then her mother shouted, her voice tight, "What have you done with Mellie?"

Charlotte joined her in front of the empty cage. "I didn't do anything. I gave him water just like you said. I found him at the bottom of the cage."

"What did you *do* to him?"

It wasn't like the bird was human. Charlotte adopted a grim expression. "Sometimes bad things happen and we don't know why."

Her mother looked like she wanted to slap her, and Charlotte was afraid she might. Instead, Elisha lifted the cage from the wood stool and slammed it down again. The parakeet's bar jumped. The water bottle crashed to the cage bottom. Birdseed flew everywhere. *"Where is he?"*

"I buried him," she said, because it was what her mother wanted to hear. From the look on her mother's face, Charlotte could tell Elisha didn't believe her but chose to let it go, reluctant for the time being to learn how Charlotte actually had disposed of the bird.

Closing her eyes, Elisha rested her head against the cage. When she raised her forehead, it was imprinted with the pattern of the bars.

~~~~~~~~~~

Charlotte had kept the cotton twill golf cap her father was wearing when he died. The hospital returned it in a green plastic bag with his clothes, shoes, and wallet. It was easy enough to claim the cap as her own in the days before the bird came into the house, when gauze seemed to cover her mother's eyes, and Elisha answered anything Charlotte said with "Yes, honey."

"I'm going to blow my brains out now," Charlotte said once, testing her.

"Yes, honey."

The sides of the cap came over her ears; the brim reached her eyes. A ring of sweat darkened the inside. The cotton bore the metallic odor of his mineral sunscreen. Charlotte didn't go to church. She didn't know if she believed in God. But she felt the cap was holy because the sweat, the lotion, and stray black hairs trapped in the metal buckle contained remnants of her father.

Behind her closed bedroom door, she slipped it on. "Flex your knees, Charlie," her father used to say when he stood over her at the tee. Clapping, he said, "*Bull's*-eye," when she hit it straight. "Let's grab a beer," they would chime as they headed back to the clubhouse, though they both knew she would get a milkshake. Surrounded by acres of manicured grass, her father, long-legged and confident at her side, Charlotte felt she had won a prize. It never occurred to her that luck was fragile, capable of vanishing in an afternoon. She had pictured her future as a pro, signing autographs for young girls. Now she refused to go anywhere near a course.

Sitting on the carpet, she yanked the bill down and murmured, "Fore," wishing she could go back and warn her father. She touched her temple.

Charlotte heard her mother in the den, rattling the cage as she cleaned it, and she remembered how the bird would shake the bars, searching for an escape. She wouldn't miss the metal clattering in the afternoon, but she didn't like seeing her mother so distressed.

Later that night, she and her mother sat down to dinner in the kitchen. Elisha had changed into old shorts and a black tank top, and her hair knot was unraveling. Briefly, Charlotte missed the mother who had dressed up for the bird. "I'm sending you back to Dr. Birnbaum," Elisha said.

Charlotte speared a chicken breast on her fork and waved it at her mother. "You know chicken is a bird, right?"

Her mother smacked a serving spoon filled with mashed potatoes onto Charlotte's plate, spraying white clouds across the table.

This was what Charlotte remembered from her previous three therapy sessions: the doctor's soccer ball belly pressing against his Oxford shirt and a white noise machine that couldn't fill the endless silences.

~~~~~~~~

After Charlotte pulled on her father's golf cap at school the next morning, kids parted around her in the hall. When her father died, all the news stations had carried it. Hats were not allowed in school, but no one objected to her wearing one.

"Charlotte! I've been meaning to talk to you." Mr. Marcus, the golf coach, hurried toward her. It was too late to duck into a classroom or the stairwell. He wore a team shirt and carried a clipboard, his tan skin thick as a hide. "How you doin', Charlotte?"

"I'm not playing anymore." But his presence made her think about it. How good it felt to hit a long drive, to sink a putt.

"I'm not asking about golf. I'm asking how you're doing. In life."

"Great. My father's dead and my mother's insane. I'm doing great."

"Sorry to hear that." Mr. Marcus told Charlotte for the umpteenth time how much he admired her father, how he'd followed his career from when Mellie was a junior. "Listen, I'm putting together a trip to Colorado. Nice and cool there. Just a fun trip. No drills, just play. How about you come?"

It would be like returning to the scene of a crime. "I can't."

"Just think about it."

"I have to go. I'll be late for class."

"Deposit's due next Tuesday!" he called after her, as she started down the hall.

Charlotte was the team's top golfer. At her father's funeral, her teammates had stared at the bleak mortuary carpet or the blown-up photo of her father that rested on an easel. Anywhere but at Charlotte's face. They wished her "condolences," said her father "was in a better place" and that she'd "be reunited with him in heaven," words adults had poured into their mouths. After the funeral, she didn't hear from them. Not one.

"They feel uncomfortable. Give them time," her mother said.

"*They're* uncomfortable?" Charlotte stripped the team photo from her bedroom wall.

~~~~~~~~

Charlotte rode the bus to the doctor's office after school. Nothing had changed in the waiting room. When she sat in a leather and chrome chair, her feet dangled above the floor. Hanging on the walls were photographs of roadrunners. At least the place had air-conditioning. She was early.

Among the magazines on an end table was a *Golf Digest* special issue on the Masters Tournament. From the date, she could tell her father had been alive when it came out. She looked through it, so absorbed she didn't hear the door to the office open. A client wearing tennis shoes and a visor shuffled out.

"You can have it," the doctor said to Charlotte as he motioned for her to come in. She stuffed the magazine into her backpack under a notebook and a bruised apple.

The doctor held a white pad and a plastic ballpoint pen, the kind that came a dozen to a box and dried out if you left the cap off. Black socks bunched at his pale ankles. He settled into his armchair. "Your mother told me there was a problem with a parakeet."

Charlotte sat opposite him on the edge of the couch. "It was hot. She didn't fix the air-conditioning. The bird died of the heat."

The doctor made a note. He scratched his ankle with the back of his pen. "That must have made you feel terrible."

She tried without success to read what the doctor had written. Sawing the seam of her jeans with her nail, she opened a small hole. She didn't know how she felt about the bird. She hadn't thought she cared, but the night before, she had dreamed about parakeets, dozens of pastel birds encased in miniature coffins. And that morning, over breakfast, the house had been terribly quiet, her mother speaking in hushed tones when she spoke at all. Charlotte poked her finger into the seam and widened the hole.

The doctor's ballpoint had begun to leak, staining his fingers.

"Why don't you get a better pen?"

As he rummaged in his desk drawer, Charlotte found herself hoping he would bring out a silver pen that was cold and smooth, a pen with character, knowing at the same time he wouldn't.

He retrieved another crummy ballpoint and threw the other away. "How's that?"

The loss came back to her—her mother pulling her out of class a week after the accident to say her father had died. Charlotte had been to see him only once. His eyes stayed closed the entire visit. As she laid her hand over his, a machine sucked thick breaths for him, another beeped the rhythm of his heart.

Outside the school, she and her mother sat in the car. A radio DJ talked about a new pizza chain. Loudspeaker announcements and class bells floated in through the open windows, while her old life, with her father at its center, floated out. Even if Charlotte wanted to tell the doctor *how that was*, she couldn't. The muscles in her face had gone slack. She bent down and pretended to look for something in her backpack, hoping the doctor wouldn't notice her hands shaking.

When she got home, Charlotte changed from the ripped jeans into shorts.

Sitting at the desk in her bedroom later that day, she told her mother, "I'm not going back to the doctor."

"Yes, you are." Her mother plucked the torn jeans from the floor.

The magazine Charlotte had taken from the doctor's office was spread out before her, along with dozens of other golf magazines her father had kept. She had gone through them and cut out her father's image and now she had piles of him, driving, putting, riding in a cart. "Seeing the doctor won't help. He doesn't know anything about me."

Her mother sat on the unmade bed. "Then you'll have to fill him in. You can start by telling him what happened to Mellie."

"*You* don't see a shrink."

Examining the ripped jeans, her mother said, "Maybe I should."

Charlotte stared at her. "What would you talk to him about?"

Her mother shrugged.

"I think you cared more about the bird than about Dad."

"I can care about more than one thing."

~~~~~~~~~

Charlotte and her mother ate dinner at the mall to escape the heat. The air-conditioning at the house was still broken. After the meal, they strolled past an ice-cream shop. Names of a dozen flavors were painted in pastel colors on the window, and the smell of a freshly pressed waffle cone drifted out the door. Charlotte remembered the kid behind the counter growing exasperated when her father wanted to sample every flavor. "How else will I know which is best?" her father had asked, tiny plastic spoons accumulating in his large hand, while Charlotte hid behind her mother, pretending not to know him. Now she wished she'd tried all those flavors with him.

Three women in shorts and sneakers powered by, step counters on their wrists and plastic water bottles in their hands. Regret lodged in Charlotte's chest. What a small thing it would have been to give the bird water.

A man wheeled a toddler in a stroller. Outside a toy-shop window, the boy pointed and said, "Truck," and the man repeated it.

"Ollipop," said the boy, as they passed a candy store.

"Lollipop," the man corrected, bending to dust bangs from the boy's eyes and kiss him on the forehead.

Charlotte watched, unable to turn away, until the pair disappeared into a restaurant. She wondered how long the boy would have his father and how he would lose him. When her mother took her hand, she didn't object.

In a pet-shop window, a parakeet cocked its head. "Is this where you got him?"

"He was supposed to cheer you up."

"It was like you were gone, too," Charlotte said to her mother's reflection.

"I know."

Charlotte leaned forward, her fingers smudging the glass. The bird had a blush of red feathers on its face and green markings on its wings. Charlotte saw other birds, too, but none of them was Mellie, who was buried, wings ruffled and dirty, under chicken bones and mashed potatoes. Parakeets, cockatiels, and African grays, seeds and pellets, screeches and chirps, filled the store. Charlotte turned away, dragging her mother along, birds continuing to flutter before her eyes. When they came to an exit, she pulled Elisha through, welcoming the ferocious blast of heat that made it impossible to think or remember.

When Charlotte got home from school the next day, she saw her mother's Lexus parked in the garage, though Elisha should have been at work. Charlotte called out to her in the house and then went outside and discovered her mother sifting through a bag of trash. It had been three days since Charlotte had disposed of Mellie, and the garbage truck was due any minute.

From the tops of fences, crows cawed to one another over the whirr of a compressor. The air-conditioning had been fixed.

Her mother had rested the garbage bag on the ground. Next to it lay a trowel. "Try the other one," she said to Charlotte, looking toward a second bag that was still in the container. Charlotte set that bag next to the first. She kneeled and uncinched the tie before thrusting in her hands. She felt the parakeet before she saw him, just where she had buried him, and lifted him up. His feathers stuck out in clumps. With a crumpled napkin, she tried to wipe off jelly, coffee grounds, and potatoes, but succeeded only in working the mess deeper into his feathers. Closing her eyes, she saw his wings beating, heard him singing a nineties pop song. But of course when she opened her eyes, the bird was as still as ever. It was too late for anything she once could have done. Charlotte tried to hand Mellie to her mother, but Elisha passed her the trowel instead. The bird was Charlotte's now.

L'Chaim

~~~~~~~~~~~~~~
~~~~~~~~

No music accompanied Lila Orr's entrance into the deserted hallway of her parents' home. No one played the famous wedding march that she and Morris Hirsch had settled on after deciding they were too old to get married to the Rolling Stones.

The musician had left hours before. From experience he could tell the difference between the jitters and a decision reached in the eleventh hour that the thing was better off not done. He had packed up his organ and congratulated himself on getting paid in advance. Lila's parents had retired to their bedroom, her father still sniffing the cigar he'd planned to smoke during the reception.

Silk shoe straps hooked over two fingers, Lila stepped into the yard to find the corgis humping under the *chuppah* and the cat cleaning its fur. She walked barefoot down the aisle on rose petals whose edges had begun to blacken. Lila waited for the dogs to finish and then picked up Molly, the female. It helped to hold something alive as she surveyed the elegant wreckage.

Twenty rows of white wooden chairs populated the lawn. To rent a chair for twenty-four hours cost five dollars. Was it possible she had spent a year of her life on such things?

Holding the dog under one arm, she snapped a few pictures with her phone. She wanted desperately to forget the day, but there would be times when she might want to remember it. Refusing to come out of the study was the bravest thing she had ever done. Better to have said no two years before on Coney Island when Morris presented the two-carat ring in a clamshell that still smelled like the sea. Morris's voice was just as nasal then; he had the same habit of correcting her. Better to have broken it off then. But not as brave as breaking it off now, bringing humiliation on herself and Morris, and risking her father having a heart attack among his accounting partners and golf buddies.

She wondered what had happened to all the food (forty-five dollars per person for plated grilled salmon and vegetables, an organic locally grown salad). Did the caterer take it down to the shelter, her instructions for the leftovers? She could have eaten a whole salmon. Three pieces of wedding cake with buttercream icing. She was that hungry.

Relief overshadowed her embarrassment. For the first time in days—since her final fitting, she realized—her lungs expanded to fill her chest. She noticed the scent of crab-apple blossoms and the breeze caressing her neck (her hair was still pinned). It was spring and she was alive and she would not marry Morris. The Pottery Barn goblet that was to be crushed under Morris's heel as part of the ceremony sat on a small table next to a bottle of Manischewitz. She set the dog down, broke the seal on the wine, and filled the glass. The glass would not be broken, not that afternoon, maybe never. "*L'chaim*," she said to herself, "to life."

A Cat Called Grievous

~~~~~~~~~~
~~~~~

In the end we were a family. Not like yours, maybe, but one that suited us, and we stayed together a long time. Like most families, we began with two. Then, when Weldon and I had been married for seven years, he discovered the cat, curled inside a fleece-lined boot on our porch. We could have named her Boot.

"Eugenia, come see her," he called. Excitement saturated his voice, which was ordinarily tentative.

The boot lay on its side. The cat was hidden, all but her face, a mass of black fur with a streak of blond down her nose and yellow eyes. Hiding places were plentiful on the porch—boxes half filled with newspapers to be recycled, empty planter pots—but nothing as warm as the boot.

"She's had a litter," Weldon said after she crawled out, teats stretched like putty and hanging low. His lips trembled, and I thought he might cry.

I took his hand, squeezed the rangy fingers, rubbed a thick knuckle with my thumb. Under other circumstances, we would have called her Mama.

Her kittens were gone, eaten by coyotes, perhaps. Every day she prowled through snowdrifts that hid the withered Colorado landscape, wailing as she searched for them. She returned at night, wet fur pasted down, shivering. Ignoring the bowl of warm milk and plate of sardines we put out, she crawled into the boot.

After a week, she stopped going out. She sat on the porch, long neck stretched toward a shark-gray sky, howling for hours. We called her Grievous.

Another snow fell. It topped Weldon's tractor-trailer, and the hulking machine loomed even larger. Thick flakes swirled around the house, stuck to the windows in clumps, and slid down leaving watery trails. Drifts buried the boot. Grievous crouched behind a box on the porch, taking shelter from the wind.

"What do you think?" Weldon asked. "Should we let her in?" I nodded. He held the door open, jiggling the knob. It was his nature to feel rejected, so I knew he was concerned she would refuse us. As I backed up, clearing a path, she crept in and settled under the sofa.

In the room we called the nursery, its pale pink walls stenciled with sheep, I slipped a mattress from the empty crib. Above, a black-and-white solar system hung cobwebby and desolate. On the opposite side of the room stood a dusty changing table and a dresser that had never been used.

"What are you doing?" Weldon asked from the doorway, his voice wavering.

"Grievous can sleep on it."

"What about the baby?"

"What baby?"

I tucked the mattress in a corner of our bedroom, a luxurious cat bed, but Grievous ignored it.

A few days later, I sawed a hole in the front door and covered it with a rubber flap. Grievous came and went as she pleased, while at a nearby worktable I stitched dresses and tailored suits. I paused each time I heard the slap of the rubber, glad she had her freedom, relieved when she returned.

We took her to the vet to be spayed. As I lugged the cat carrier, I imagined it was a bassinet. I thought a baby would coo pleasantly, but the cat moaned, protesting her abduction.

"Too many cats already," the vet said, smiling in a way that told me she enjoyed extracting reproductive organs and mopping up blood. She was small and energetic, with pointy ears, like a bat.

The steel examination table shone, and I had second thoughts about interfering with nature. Grievous had lost one litter already. Afterward, I admired the neat cuts the doctor had made.

Grievous recovered and hurtled through our neighborhood, pouncing on mice and chipmunks. Outside our dining-room window, she caught a rabbit. Her head vanished inside the creature and then reappeared, pink intestinal pasta dripping from her whiskers.

"She's something, isn't she?" I said.

"You want me to take a picture?" Weldon asked.

He was joking, but I did. If not to display, then to keep in my wallet, a reminder of nature's ferocity, which I admired. Yet it seemed indecent. I shook my head no.

Weldon wrapped his long arm around my shoulders, pulling me to him. I remembered the way he had comforted me early in our marriage when I failed to get pregnant, telling me that without a child we could continue in the way of newlyweds. "We won't have to share our bed," he said. "At least not for a little while." He kissed my eyelids, throwing me into a welcome darkness. Unbuttoning his shirt, I grasped his springy black chest hair, pearled his nipple between my teeth. I mounted him on the couch, pleasure erasing our disappointment.

Back then when he was on the road, hauling dry goods to Mississippi and New Jersey, he'd call me when my favorite song, Shania Twain's "Any Man of Mine," came on the radio. We'd sing it together, road noise backing up his airy voice. He enjoyed the weight of the truck beneath him and how responsive it was. Rarely did he return home without a gift, not from gas-station shops, but from boutiques he had ferreted out in unfamiliar towns—an antique perfume atomizer, rare fabrics for my work, a picture of the two of us inked on a grain of rice. In those days, I greeted his return with the delight of a young child.

In the spring after Grievous came, Weldon and I took walks after dinner. We struggled to find things to say to each other, the years having exhausted our best stories. How many times could I hear that Weldon had nearly drowned in a reservoir when he was eight, discovering too late that the shore had receded and his friends had abandoned him? He already knew I had been expelled from high school for puncturing the fuel tank on an English teacher's car after she gave me an *F*. We remarked on the weather and the damage winter had done to the roads.

One evening, we passed a toddler riding a tricycle in front of our house. In a neighboring yard, a Doberman hurled itself against the chain that secured it to a tree. We had gone only a few steps when the chain snapped and the dog leaped onto the child, knocking him from his seat. The dog lunged for the boy's soft neck, and the child screamed. Before we could reach them, Grievous appeared and vaulted onto the dog's back, raking claws through its hide. The dog spun from boy to cat. We grabbed the toddler and ran inside, while Grievous escaped up a tree.

The next night, the child's mother brought Grievous a pot of catnip, setting it on our porch. She pulled a tissue from her pocket and blew her nose. "He cracked a tooth in the fall and his palms were bloody, but thanks to you and your cat, he's alive. He's my only child. You can't imagine what it's like."

What did she mean by that? I pushed the plastic pot toward her with my foot. "Grievous doesn't like catnip."

"We're just glad she could help," Weldon said and led me inside.

~~~~~~~~~

Our house was large, with three bedrooms in addition to the nursery, a playroom, and a formal dining room. It was crammed with heavy furniture, heirloom secretaries, and mahogany dining and bedroom sets. Before Grievous, it had felt empty.

We had planned to have a large family. Weldon and I were only children, and we had inherited all our parents' material goods and all their hopes. My father had been an astronomer, and I fantasized about girls in velvet jackets winning the science fair and curly-haired boys discovering stars they named after us. But after years of noting my temperature on a chart, of harvesting and implanting and miscarrying, I gave up. Not so with Weldon, who continued to hope for a miracle.

"Maybe we should sell the house. Get a condo," I had said over breakfast, the last time science failed us. I scraped charcoal from my toast with a knife, raining black ash onto the pine table.

"Kids need room to play." Weldon drowned his oatmeal in milk and rowed a spoon through the mush.

"Something modern." I bit into the dry toast.

When Grievous joined our household, I forgot about a condo. I hated to imagine her trapped in three small rooms, a litter box wedged between the tub and the toilet, and no access to the outdoors. In our house she had free rein. I fed her in the kitchen, brushed her in the living room, and in the bedroom talked to her in that high singsong reserved for babies. No matter that she sharpened her claws on the legs of the eighteenth-century armoire and sliced the thick tweed on the settee. We hadn't selected these elegant furnishings ourselves, after all.

Weldon seldom called me from the road anymore. But one night, as he was piloting his tractor trailer on three hours' sleep and chomping microwaved cheeseburgers from 7-Eleven, I heard from him. "Could you check if I set the DVR to record the hockey games?" he said, though I knew he would never forget that.

"Let me see," I told him, and stood before the recorder for the time it would have taken to press the right buttons. "All done." I waited for him to get to the real reason for his call.

"Remember to take your prenatal vitamins," he said as if he had just thought of it. He set them out for me every morning when he was home.

"Right," I said. I almost laughed. Except for one occasion of frustrated, side-by-side masturbation, we hadn't had sex in nearly two months.

I no longer bristled when clients ordered dresses for christenings and bar mitzvahs. Bold darts flew from the waists and bosoms I sewed. Grievous hopped into my lap at night, softening everything: the armchair, the roar of a passing motorbike, the tick of my pulse. But after a few minutes she grew impatient, wriggled to the floor, and licked off my scent.

She slipped out each morning. I didn't know where she went, though once I saw her drinking from a concrete birdbath. Afternoons she ascended a giant oak, sprawled on a high branch, and spied on prey.

"You want me to call the fire department?" a neighbor asked, as the sun set, and Grievous remained in the tree. An elderly woman with ropy arms who always hosted three generations at holiday meals, she knew nothing about cats.

"Best time for hunting," I said.

I thought Grievous was indestructible, but one day she was hit by a Corvette. We heard the *whump* of the impact, followed by a cry of rage. Her femur had fractured, and the bone jutted through skin. Unsure if she would survive, we raced her to the vet. The doctor pinned the bone and sewed her up. The accident shook us from our routine. That night, we cradled Grievous and each other.

After she fell asleep, we tiptoed to another bedroom. "Do you think we'll wake her?" I asked, but we were already shedding our flannel pajamas. I didn't think I could become pregnant.

~~~~~~~~~

Six months later, we scrubbed the nursery, and Weldon hung the needlework he had bought in an arts-and-crafts shop in Nebraska: "Welcome Baby." Grievous wove between the legs of the crib, marking them with her scent. She rolled on the beige carpet, seeding it with black fur.

She had slept in our bed since the accident. "We might want the baby in bed with us," Weldon said that night. He pulled the covers to his chin and flipped the TV to a show about prisoners. Grievous tapped his hand, but Weldon refused to pet her.

"There's room for all of us." Sitting at a table across the room, I cut out letters of the alphabet for a quilt. The sex of the baby was still a mystery. I pictured a perfect, pink-cheeked infant like the ones on baby food jars, bundled in the quilt.

"She might scratch the baby."

The utility knife slipped, and I sliced off the top of the *W*. "She wouldn't. Not intentionally." I had grown large and hated to bend down, so I didn't bother to retrieve the severed fabric.

"Grievous won't mind. She's always been very independent." Since Weldon had learned he was becoming a father, an unwelcome confidence had crept into his manner.

I tried to object, but he lowered Grievous to the floor.

She didn't fit on my lap anymore, and I was too tired to hold her in my arms. I had been having trouble sleeping. Every night, just as I was about to doze off, the baby would kick, waking me. During the day, I nodded over my sewing machine, wearing the only clothes that fit me, tentlike dresses I made myself. My nails grew so fast they were like claws no matter how often I cut them.

~~~~~~~~~~

We brought the child home, a girl named Neda. Weldon juggled diapers and a bassinet, while I hobbled into the house, aching where the baby had torn me, resisting her entry into the world.

"I wonder where Grievous is," I said. I felt an inexplicable longing for her.

Weldon stroked Neda's cheek, stared into her gray eyes, and cooed.

"I'm sure the cat's fine," he said.

The baby cried, a grating sound. Her face flushed. I took off my coat and lifted my blouse.

At night her bawling woke me from dreams in which a companion and I dined on herring in cream sauce and salmon fillets. Because I was deprived of sleep, my work suffered. Seams veered right and left, unraveled behind missing knots. Erratic cuts ruined bolts of fabric. I left pins in hems and delivered a wedding dress to a man celebrating his fiftieth anniversary.

I would lay Neda on the couch while I worked, admiring the thin auburn curl I had arranged in the center of her otherwise bald, floppy head. Baby acne dotted her face, fat pooched her cheeks, and she stuck out her tongue. She didn't look like a girl who would one day win a science fair.

We saw only brief glimpses of Grievous, but evidence of her was everywhere: scratches on the nursery door, bite marks on the crib, and mice piled high on the porch, babies that looked more stunned than dead.

One night we heard the childlike wailing of a cat fight. A redhaired EMT who lived down the block said she was coming home from an emergency call and saw Grievous swipe a bobcat.

The owner of the Corvette, a televangelist whose megachurch was blocks from our house, claimed Grievous slashed his tires. He sped through the neighborhood without regard for pets or children and had been the one to injure Grievous. "I saw her sniffing around the car," he said, "and the next day they were flat."

I could tell Weldon suspected me because of the English teacher, but didn't have the heart to accuse his wife. I let him believe what he wanted.

How I missed the days when Grievous would snake around my legs while I pedaled the sewing machine. Feeling the gentle pressure of her body, my heart had expanded, and I understood what it meant to love without words. Neda woke screaming from her nap, and I trudged off to change her.

~~~~~~~~~~

The little girl grew. When he was home, Weldon sat on the floor with her, plucking a toy piano while she sang "Twinkle Twinkle" off-key. He tried to teach her the sounds of the animals, but she declared *moo* when she should have cried *baa* and quacked when she should have roared. When he counted on her fingers, she poked him in the eye. She fell asleep on his lap, listening to stories of his childhood on a Colorado ranch.

But he was often away, and then it was just the child and me.

One day, as she played on the living-room floor, she pointed under the breakfront and squealed, "Kitty, Mama!"

Grievous sauntered out and circled Neda.

I paused in my sewing. "Good kitty." I hadn't seen her in a long time and was relieved she looked healthy, eyes clear and coat shining.

"Good kitty," Neda said.

Grievous stepped onto the child's lap. Her claws were like scythes. Brushing Neda's arm, they carved lines in blood.

"Oh dear." I wiped the blood with a fabric swatch.

"Oh dear," Neda said.

Grievous purred. I had forgotten what a soothing sound that was and closed my eyes to listen.

Neda trailed the cat all afternoon, over couches, under beds and armoires. Dust bunnies clung to her hair, her jumper blackened. When I lay her down for an afternoon nap in the bed we had just bought her, she called for Grievous. The cat ambled across the nursery floor and jumped in bed. I was glad they were getting along.

That night, I set a plate of tuna casserole in front of Neda, and she spooned half onto the floor for Grievous. After the cat ate, she cleaned herself, licking her paws and rubbing her face. Copying her, my daughter smeared spit on her cheeks.

Grievous disappeared through the cat door, and Neda tried to follow. She jammed her head through, but her shoulders got stuck. As I pulled her inside, she swatted my hands. She yelled for the cat and was inconsolable, weeping so hard she wheezed. The next night was the same. Not for the first time, I thought how much easier it was to love a creature whose habit was silence.

When Weldon returned a few days later, he sealed the cat door, trapping Grievous inside. We watched from a few feet away, Grievous and I. "It's wrong," I said. "She's wild."

"You're the one who complained Neda was upset," he said through the nails in his mouth. I should have known he would do anything for the child.

~~~~~~~~~

I had always read to my daughter before bed, but now she shoved *Pinocchio* and *The Velveteen Rabbit* aside and patted her belly, insisting I scratch it. When I did, she murmured, a throaty hum. I liked to imagine she was Grievous's littermate, a second cat we had rescued from the snow. Grievous slept under the covers, her tail in Neda's face.

Perched on the window ledge, Grievous stared at finches. She stalked a squirrel, lifting her paw to trap it, but it was Grievous who was trapped on the wrong side of the glass. She crept behind Neda, who was unaware of being followed. I couldn't help but admire the cat's stealthy movements, the way she rotated her ears to pick up every sound. They played together, and Neda shrieked and laughed.

So what if the child never went to the park or McDonald's anymore—she howled if separated from Grievous—or if I had to put her plate on the floor next to the cat's to get her to eat? She could learn a lot from Grievous.

"Do you know she pees in the cat box?" As he interrogated me, Weldon held up a diaper Neda had torn off.

I suppose he would have preferred a more helpless child. "It's easier than changing her."

He shook his head and closed his eyes. I could tell he feared he no longer understood his daughter.

When he tried to get Neda to play, to pummel the towers he erected from blocks or to gaze at the moon through a plastic telescope, she refused. "Play Grievous," she said, and off she went.

Sometimes Grievous lay on the floor, feet splayed behind, content to let Neda brush her. But I found bite marks on Neda when I bathed her. Grievous could be savage, but Neda didn't seem to mind.

My daughter no longer clung to my apron or watched me sew. Gone were the days of her reaching for the shiny blade when I cut leather and vinyl. She was off with Grievous, napping in sunbeams and chasing flies. She raked the furniture with her sharp nails and curled in a ball to sleep, her head hidden in her hands.

One day I heard snarling and yowling. When I went to investigate, I found Neda on the floor of the nursery. Scratches ran the length of her neck and hands, and her forehead was bloody. Fur erect, back arched, Grievous commanded the bed.

"Kitty won't let me up," the child whimpered. When I approached, Grievous hissed. I cleaned Neda up and tucked her into my bed. Despite their fight, Neda called for Grievous to join her.

When Weldon returned from his trip and saw Neda's injuries, he waited until the child was asleep and kicked the cat's bowl across the kitchen. "We're getting rid of her."

"Who, Neda?" I joked.

His mouth tightened.

"Neda would never forgive us," I said. I couldn't imagine life without Grievous. She was our first, and I wouldn't give her up.

"We'll tell her Grievous ran away."

"It's not the cat's fault. You trapped her inside."

When Grievous padded into the room, Weldon lunged for her, but she scrambled to the top of a bookcase. While he dragged over a stepladder, she dropped to the floor, dashed behind the refrigerator, and then vanished into the basement.

Weldon put out a fresh dish of cat food and watched it, but Grievous waited until we slept to eat. The next day he built a trap, cutting a hole in a wood chest and rigging a door to shut when the cat went for the tuna inside. He caught only Neda's arm.

When he went back on the road, things changed. I lured Grievous with her favorite foods—raw chicken liver and kidneys—and we became a family again. She and Neda batted blocks around the floor, and I massaged Grievous with my toes.

Weldon phoned from the highway; I said I hadn't seen Grievous.

The cat's ears rotated toward the front of the house when Weldon's truck rolled over the asphalt. As soon as he opened the door, she darted out. "Good riddance," he shouted. When he turned back to me, he looked tired, as if he could barely carry his suitcase.

Neda tried to follow the cat, but Weldon clasped her arm with his free hand. "No more Grievous," he said.

She sank her teeth into his fingers, and he drew them to his chest, his eyes narrowing. As she fled from the room, he dropped the suitcase, and it toppled onto its side.

That night, I slept with the covers over my face, missing Grievous, who had lain against me while Weldon was away.

Sitting on the couch the next morning, Weldon clutched a cup of coffee he'd brewed from a stolen motel packet in one hand, his other hand bandaged and resting on a pile of unread newspapers in his lap. "Sometimes I think you love that cat more than you love me."

Distracted, I plunged the sewing machine needle through my middle finger. While Weldon drove me to the emergency room, I considered all Grievous had given me and how little she had asked in return.

Neda lay on her bed, refusing to eat or play. She yowled in her sleep, her arms and legs churning as if she were running on all fours. Half-moons darkened beneath her eyes.

Snow fell. I saw Grievous take shelter under Weldon's tractor-trailer. I was glad she had found a dry spot. After dark, Neda and I snuck out with sardines. We kneeled in the snow at the edge of the trailer, huddling together for warmth, and I set down the plate. Grievous allowed us to stroke her ears as she ate.

A week went by, and Weldon left again. He was headed to Missouri but made it only half a mile. Receiving a call about the accident, I remembered the gentle way he had with Neda and the happiness of our early days. I would miss him. The police officer told me his brake lines had been compromised—four neat slashes all in a row—and they tore as he rounded an icy curve. The semi careened down an embankment, landing in a ravine. Weldon died instantly.

Neda and I were glad to have Grievous back. I unsealed the cat door, and we watched her through the window, hijacking a house finch and biting the head off of a squirrel. I bought a taxidermy kit. We stuffed the trophies she left us and mounted them on the walls of the nursery after painting over the sheep.

Better Homes and Gardens

~~~~~~~~~~
~~~~~

Neal pulled up to a small ranch house with a cracked concrete drive, a pizza-delivery sign gripping the roof of his silver BMW. He rang the bell twice and was about to turn around when a boy of perhaps ten opened the door.

"My mom said to tell you we can't pay for it." The kid stood with one bare foot on the other. He had curly black hair Neal imagined girls would one day run their fingers through.

"I'm guessing it was you that called."

"Number's on the fridge."

Neal could cover it, but where did that end? He'd never been especially charitable. It would be odd to start now when he was neglecting his own family. The consulting firm that had employed him for the past decade had folded three months before, and since then he'd made no effort to find a real job. It was 2008, and hardly anyone was hiring. But even if they had been, he wouldn't have looked. He'd come to hate that kind of work. The endless pressure to generate revenue and the constant jockeying within the firm had caused his blood pressure to soar and aggravated his eczema, angry patches spreading across his back and hands, resisting prescription creams and hypnotherapy. When the firm went bankrupt, he'd secretly celebrated.

The boy touched the red Mama Jane's delivery bag.

"What's your name?" Neal asked.

"Caleb."

"I can't give this to you. You know that, right? That's not how it works. Mama Jane has to get paid. Otherwise there are no more pies." It was a crock. Caleb looked like he knew it, too, narrowing his eyes and shaking his head. What was one pizza?

Inside the house, a woman bent to gather some kind of cards and a PlayStation from the carpet. Younger than Neal's wife, Tara, she wore loose jeans and a "Will Code for Beer" T-shirt. She was all angles, shoulder blades and knees jutting against fabric. Neal liked how little there was of her. He almost changed his mind about giving the boy the pizza.

"You're letting in bugs," the woman said to Caleb.

As Neal drove back to the shop, air-conditioning chilled his neck and ankles, bringing goose bumps to his skin. A lifetime supply of mint gum filled a 7-Eleven bag on the floor. His girls, Allie and Avery, sophomores at Long Island Prep, inhaled the stuff. Used pieces wrapped in foil sparkled beneath the seats, tumbled across the carpet when he took a sharp turn, flattened beneath his sneakers.

That morning, he had withdrawn five thousand dollars from his and Tara's account. Now he opened the glove box, glanced at the loose stack of hundreds, and thought again about escaping: renting a cabin in the Poconos, leaving his phone behind. Tara would be furious if she knew about the money. The thought made him smile.

He remembered how angry she'd been when she first saw the delivery sign. "It's a gag, right? It's not enough for us to be poor, you want to humiliate me, too?"

Maybe he did. After he was laid off, he was using her laptop—his had belonged to the firm—and he discovered dozens of Facebook messages to Lincoln Moran, who listed his home as Milwaukee. Tara had gone to high school with Lincoln, and it was only out of boredom that Neal began to read their communications. At first, Tara wrote to Lincoln about her mother's deteriorating health and Avery's learning disabilities. But later, Neal himself became the subject of her messages. Always working, he had no time for her or the girls, she wrote; he didn't appreciate what it took to run their home. Tara and Lincoln exchanged phone numbers. Then the messages ended. Neal examined their cell-phone bills and found calls to and from Lincoln, as many as three a day. Neal never would have suspected because Tara paid the household bills. Tara had hearted every one of Lincoln's Facebook posts, even the one about a missing dog. From Tara's account, Neal blocked Lincoln. If he couldn't hit the guy, he could at least make his bloated face and tweed cap disappear.

"Hear from Wisconsin today?" he asked Tara, when she returned from the supermarket.

Pink splotches bloomed on her cheeks. She lowered overflowing cloth bags to the floor, ignoring an orange that rolled under a chair. "I needed someone to talk to."

Neal was sitting at the kitchen table, staring at an issue of *Sports Car Market*.

"I couldn't get your attention," she said. "You were always traveling. Even when you were home, you were texting or e-mailing clients."

"What about Lincoln, does he travel? Come to Long Island for business or maybe for pleasure?" He turned the page.

"He never touched me."

Neal thought about all the times he hadn't been able to reach Tara, afternoons she claimed she was at the spa or hadn't heard her phone. She'd highlighted her hair so the gray wouldn't show, started wearing spandex pants and sheer blouses, telling Neal she was tired of dressing like a mom. Neal had liked the changes, but he thought she was making them for him. She'd seemed happier. Looking back, that more than anything infuriated him. "Did you talk to him today?"

"He's a friend."

"That's not what I asked." He wanted to know whether she was having an affair but also didn't want to know because if she was, he would have to do something about it.

~~~~~~~~~~

Neal got home at ten. Tara was in bed, reading a British novel, the kind that would make an unbearably slow movie. They used to watch films like that together. "Landtech is hiring a senior manager," she said.

"I don't need help finding a job." They were spending the kids' college funds, which had lost half their value when the market crashed, but he couldn't bear the thought of returning to an office. He enjoyed being outside, instead of under fluorescent lights, breathing recycled air. When he pictured himself generating endless reports, attending pointless meetings, and kissing up to a CEO, his skin began to itch. Not crazy enough to think he could deliver pizzas forever, he was considering becoming a mail carrier or a taxi driver, but he wasn't ready to tell Tara.

She smelled of toothpaste and antiwrinkle cream. It had been months since she'd worn the Tom Ford lavender perfume he'd tucked into her stocking last Christmas. In the past, she'd worn it as an invitation. He wasn't expecting invitations from her now, not while he wasn't even looking for work, though he sometimes imagined entering her roughly, hearing her cry out. He'd always been tender.

She set the book on the nightstand and turned off the light. A halo burned around her white silk pajamas before his eyes adjusted.

He walked down the hall to his daughters' rooms, his footsteps muffled by dense wool carpet, and read the stickers on Avery's door: "Enter at your own Peril," "Quarantine Zone," and "If I Liked You, You'd Already Be Inside." Light from the room leaked out onto Neal's shoes. Allie's room was dark. He pictured Caleb illuminated by the buzzing porch lamp. Boys would have been easier or at least easier to understand. He knocked.

"What do you want?" Avery said.

"It's Dad, can I come in?" He grasped the brass doorknob. When they remodeled, Tara had bought refurbished fixtures from a workshop that employed mentally challenged adults. Each knob cost as much as a hubcap, and she filled the house with them. "Just wanted to say good night to my girl."

"I'm not dressed," Avery said, laughing in a way that made him think it wasn't true.

~~~~~~~~

"Take that thing *off*," Avery said, pointing to the pizza sign on top of the BMW.

Since Tara had returned to work as a project manager a month ago, Neal drove the girls to school. He had forgotten the sign the night before. "I'll just have to put it back later."

"I'm not riding with that thing on."

"We'll help you, Dad," Allie said.

"Speak for yourself."

It was his fault Avery was pushy. His and Tara's. Always giving the girls whatever they wanted: Game Boys when their fingers were hardly big enough to press the buttons, designer clothes they outgrew in six months, soccer camps where professionals coached. He had enjoyed spoiling them, and it was easier than saying no. Now it was too late. He knew from experience to give in, or Avery would sit on the front step refusing to move.

Wrestling with the sign, he scratched the roof of the car, cutting a jagged line through the luminous paint. "Fuck."

"Dad!" Allie said.

"I guess it's okay to say that now," Avery said. "Fuck, fuck, fuck."

The girls rode in the back as he drove to school. They used to fight to sit in front with him. He glanced at them in the rearview mirror. They were beautiful, even Avery, when she didn't know she was being watched and wasn't scowling. Skin perfect and pale like their mother's, straight black hair touched only by the world's most exclusive salon products. Avery had recently cut hers into a bob, perhaps so people would stop calling her Allie. How two such attractive girls could have come from him was a mystery.

After he dropped them off, emptiness took hold of his day. Alone in the house, he started at sounds of appliances breathing on and off, a bird smacking into a windowpane. Tara had left a printout of the Landtech job description on his desk. Skimming it, Neal felt his chest tighten. For years, he'd told Tara how unhappy he was at work.

"You know how much everyone in this family appreciates what you do," she'd said once, which was only partially true and beside the point. Eventually he'd stopped talking about it because her willingness to see him suffer compounded his pain; he questioned who he was sacrificing for.

Now he was content to let Tara support them. It was her first job since the twins were born. He wanted her to experience work in the twenty-first century, when one person was expected to do the job of two, and the day extended beyond office hours, far into the night, e-mails, texts, and phone calls arriving during the *Late Show* and after you'd gone to bed. Maybe she wouldn't have time for Facebook. He left the job description on his desk.

Tara had written a to-do list for him on monogrammed stationery. They had let go of the housekeeper, but if Tara thought he would scrub toilets or mop floors, she was mistaken. She had never done those things, instead blogging about remodeling and talking to Lincoln while the kids were in school. He crumpled the list and tossed it into the trash.

Exiting the house through the back door, he sat on the concrete stoop. Kentucky bluegrass stretched out before him. A giant silver maple shaded the patio. Along the edge of a cedar fence, he'd planted marigolds, salvias, zinnias, three kinds of tomato plants, and two kinds of squash. On his days off, he would sometimes stay in the yard until night fell, and he couldn't see his hands. No one looked for him. The only risk, that he would miss a weed or overwater a tomato. Delivering pizzas was like that, too. At worst a customer would get the wrong pie. He retrieved a kneepad from the garage and began thinning plants.

At three he picked up Avery. Allie stayed after school for chess club. Another parent would bring her home later. Neal had driven no more than half a block when Avery opened the glove box, probably looking for gum. "Holy shit," she said.

"Close that." How had he forgotten to return the cash to the envelope? His head began to throb.

"Are you a drug dealer? Is that what you do all day?"

As she was counting bills, he grabbed them, swerving and nearly hitting a parked car.

"It's cool," she said. "You can hook me up."

"Right." He shoved the money back into the glove box and banged it shut. With the back of his hand he wiped his forehead. "I'm not a drug dealer."

She found the 7-Eleven bag and began to empty it into her backpack.

"Leave some for Allie."

"Can't forget Miss Perfect. Did we win the lottery?"

"We didn't win anything. Don't tell your mother about the money."

"Why are you keeping secrets from Mom?" She opened the glove box again and fingered the bills. "Can I have a hundred?"

"No."

"You don't want me to say anything, right?"

He had raised an extortionist. He closed the glove box again, pulled his wallet from his back pocket, and handed it to her. "Take twenty. And don't tell anyone. Not even Allie."

"We don't talk to each other. She's a geek." She withdrew the money and returned the wallet. Jamming in earphones and scrolling through her phone, she ignored him for the rest of the ride.

When they got home, he offered to make her a snack.

"Yeah, Dad, some milk and cookies, because I'm three," she called over her shoulder. She couldn't seem to get away from him fast enough, slamming her bedroom door shut.

He wanted to go after her, snatch her phone, and ground her until she learned to be as polite as Allie. But Tara was always telling him to go easy on Avery, who struggled to keep up in school and had few friends.

He watched reruns of Formula 500 races until it was time to go to Mama Jane's. To get to the shop, he drove through a neighborhood of castlelike homes even bigger than his own. Swimming pools liquefied sprawling backyards. Pool houses pushed up out of the ground. Anorexic teens lay on lounge chairs, sipping sugar-free lemonade served by Central American maids. Once, when he'd delivered to one of those addresses, a man his age tipped him fifty dollars—a karma payment, Neal figured, so the man wouldn't end up like Neal.

Mama Jane wore the same thing every day: jeans dusted with flour that matched the color of her hair, and a chef's coat. "I got one for you," she'd say when he came in the door, and he'd pick up the box and the receipt. She must have wondered about the BMW and the thick, gold wedding ring, but she didn't ask.

He'd applied for the job the day after he found out about Lincoln. "Long as you don't mind your car smelling like pizza, we can use you," Mama Jane said. Neal remembered delivering pizzas the summer of his senior year in high school, sleeping until two in the afternoon, getting stoned before work, and flirting with a girl who came in for slices. When the girl learned he was starting Cornell in the fall, she waited until he made his last delivery and then blew him in his Camaro among empty soda cups and burger wrappers. "When can I start?" Neal asked Mama Jane.

If the shop owner had a family, Neal never saw them. She talked on the phone only to take orders. The place stayed open seven days a week, and she was always there. Neal wanted to ask if she found satisfaction in a life of pies and soft drinks, but they didn't have that kind of relationship.

The night was slow, and Mama Jane let him go at eight. One of the counter guys could deliver. Neal was reluctant to head home. He boxed up a plain pizza and drove it to Caleb's house.

The boy's mother opened the door. "I didn't order that."

"I thought your son might like it."

"Look, I don't have the money, and we already ate dinner." She wore the same outfit, her wet hair hanging loose.

"It's on me."

She gripped the door, poised to close it. "Is this some kind of racket? I suppose you'll be offering me free siding next."

"I didn't want to eat alone."

She glanced at his wedding ring. "Shouldn't you be eating with your wife?"

Neal shrugged. "She doesn't like pizza."

Caleb appeared, his mouth falling open when he saw the box. He hopped from one bare foot to the other.

The woman glanced at her son and took a deep breath. "I tell him not to talk to strangers."

"And never let strangers in," Caleb said.

"I tell my daughters the same. Name's Neal, by the way."

"Don't you have pizzas to deliver?"

"Just this one."

"It's getting cold." The boy was on his toes.

The woman took the box, and Neal followed her inside.

She introduced herself as Felicia, which Neal thought he remembered meant happiness in Latin. He sat across the dining-room table from her, computer parts scattered across the scratched pine. A hard drive flattened a napkin. Tara would've cleared the table and covered it with a cloth before they sat down.

Felicia explained the functions of the components. Neal didn't understand much of what she said, but he nodded. He liked smart women.

Caleb ate, holding a slice in each hand, a third resting on his plate.

"He's had ramen every night this week," Felicia said, examining a thumb drive.

"How'd you learn about computers?"

"One of those schools that advertises on cable. Improve your life with a new career. I can't complain. It was good for a few years." She took a bite of pizza, wiped her mouth with a microfiber cloth, and said she'd been fired from her job as a programmer after coming down with chronic fatigue syndrome. "They expect you to be gung ho, but I didn't have the energy anymore. I do a few computer repairs. Mostly we get by on my disability." The humidity was kinking her hair.

Neal played with a crust while he told her about being laid off from a job he hated. He hadn't intended to get into all that. But she had opened the door, talking about her illness, and it was a simple matter to walk through. Felicia nodded, thin hands resting on the table.

It was a relief to talk about it. But it heightened the reality of his predicament. "I used to be a corporate superhero. Now I'm going to destroy my wife and daughters' lives, and they don't even know it." There were many things about his new, reduced circumstances Neal preferred. Beneath the suit he'd worn and the meals of organic, grass-fed beef he'd eaten because Tara prepared them, he'd always been a jeans and T-shirt, pizza and hot dogs, kind of guy. But his family would have a hard time adapting. The knowledge troubled him but also—and he was ashamed to admit this even to himself—gave him a perverse sense of satisfaction.

~~~~~~~~~~

"Do you mind sharing how much longer you're going to be on your vacation?" Tara asked, when he returned that night. She muted Jimmy Fallon.

"I have a job," he said, though what he earned didn't cover their groceries. He peeled off his cargo shorts and dropped them on top of a full bathroom hamper.

She sat up, arranging two pillows behind her. "I suppose if you get really ambitious, you'll take on a paper route."

"We should simplify our lives. People all over the world live on less than a hundred dollars a month." But he didn't believe the life they had constructed around wealth could be reconstructed around something else.

She turned toward the TV. Gave Jimmy back his voice. The studio audience was laughing. "You want to pretend you're in Bangladesh? Do it alone," she said. "Explain to our girls why they can't get mani-pedis with their friends."

"You earn good money. We could sell the house and move to an apartment. I could get rid of the car, buy a beater for the pizza route." He didn't expect her to agree. But he didn't know what else to say, how to tell her he wouldn't work anymore for the kind of life she and the girls wanted.

"That's what you want to do? Deliver pizzas?" She was shouting. He closed the bedroom door. She hugged her legs and dropped her forehead to her knees. Her voice, softer now, sounded like it might crack. "Why aren't you looking for a real job? Because of Lincoln? I told you we only talked."

Maybe Lincoln was the reason. Or maybe Neal was never meant to live the kind of life he'd been living. Either way, he knew he should try to explain. He owed her that. She hadn't always been a person for whom wealth was important. When they first met, she was living in an Upper West Side studio with a one-eyed cat she'd rescued. But it had been years since their lives revolved around anything other than the girls and the remodel. The cat was long dead. "The corporate life isn't for me anymore," he said. She was quiet, probably waiting for him to continue, and he might have, if she hadn't let another man make her happy.

"What about your kids?" she said.

"It'll be good for them. It's about time they learned what all this really costs."

~~~~~~~~~~

Nine thirty the next morning, Neal brought Felicia croissants. She set the brown paper bag on the dining table unopened and poured him a cup of coffee in a chipped Einstein mug, topping off her own. As they sat on the couch, Neal told her about Avery's stubbornness and his struggle to treat her learning problems with medications and therapies that didn't seem to work. "I don't know how people do it. Keep it together until their kids are grown." The PlayStation was back on the floor. Neal wondered if Felicia ever smacked Caleb after she tripped over it, or because he stuck gum behind his headboard.

"Caleb has asthma. I put an inhaler in his backpack and left one with the school nurse, but I still have nightmares where he dies because he can't breathe." She tucked her legs under her and closed her eyes. A blue vein shone in her right eyelid.

"I told Tara it was her turn to support us."

"How'd she take it?"

"Not well." The house was warm and smelled of mildew. Outside, a dead bush pressed against a window. Neal wanted to dig it up, plant something green. A laptop lay disassembled on the coffee table. Neal admired Felicia's ability to reconstruct something working from the mess. "Where's Caleb's father?"

"He disappeared a few weeks after I had the baby. I didn't know him well. I liked having Caleb to myself. Until I got sick. Then I moved in with my mother. This was her house before she died."

She had raised the boy alone, and he was fine. It gave Neal something to think about, strengthened an argument he was already making to himself.

On his way to pick up Avery from school to take her to a psychologist, Neal realized the money was still in the glove box. He'd considered bringing it into the house but was afraid Tara would discover it. He pulled over, stuffed it into the bank envelope, and tucked the envelope behind the driver's side visor.

As soon as Avery got into the car, she snapped open the glove box and rummaged inside. Next she searched the center console. "Where is it?" she said.

He was starting to hate her. He still loved her, but he also hated her. "None of your business."

As he pulled into a busy intersection, Avery lowered the visor and found it.

"Leave that alone," he said.

"I need a hundred." She took down the envelope.

"You can't have it."

"It's for a friend. You don't know her."

"I'm not kidding." When he tried to seize it, she held her hand against the passenger window out of his reach. The car swerved, but he righted it. "What does your mystery friend need it for?"

"She's on the soccer team but can't afford the fees."

He felt sorry for the girl, but she wasn't his problem. Or maybe Avery was making her up. "I'm not giving your friend money. She should ask her parents."

"They don't have it. She's on scholarship."

"We don't have it, either. Maybe you haven't noticed, but I deliver pizzas."

"Maybe you haven't noticed, but I don't give a fuck."

Neal leaned over and grabbed her arm. All he was to her was a goddamn ATM. That's all he was to any of them. Tara wanted him to pay for a house straight out of *Better Homes and Gardens*. His daughters expected new cars, top-of-the-line imports, once they got their licenses. He couldn't imagine putting them through the private colleges they would choose, though he knew he was being a hypocrite, having attended an Ivy League school himself. But then, look where that had gotten him.

The sound of the impact—mashing of metal and glass, explosion of airbags—wiped out everything else. The interior flashed white. The car spun, lifted off two wheels, and bounced down again.

Neal was shoved back in his seat, eyes closed. When he opened them, the BMW faced oncoming traffic. Avery's head angled to one side, bathed in blood. Her forehead pressed against the mangled door, and her eyes were half closed, unblinking. The side airbag hadn't deployed. Neal smelled burning metal and rubber. He wanted to reach out to Avery but was afraid.

The bank envelope was at her feet, intact. Neal lifted it and crammed it into his pocket. Even amid the chaos, he realized he might need it.

Later, after an ER doctor examined and released him, after an officer cited him for reckless driving and he called a criminal lawyer, Neal stood trembling next to his daughter's hospital bed, horrified at what he had done. He had nearly killed her. She had broken her shoulder and three ribs. Her hair was a patchwork, shaved in half a dozen places where the doctors stitched her scalp. A jagged cut furrowed her right cheek. He held himself accountable for each and every injury. When a nurse came in to adjust the IV, Neal stared at Avery's blanket, ashamed. Taking in his daughter's injuries, he couldn't help but feel his family would be better off without him.

Tara sat on a chair on the opposite side of the bed, clutching Avery's hand. Asleep under a heavy dose of painkillers, Avery didn't know how she looked. When she found out, she would blame him for destroying her life, for every glance she would get that was curious rather than admiring. He blamed himself. When he'd reached for her arm, the light turned red, but he didn't see it and continued into the intersection. An SUV rammed the passenger side of the BMW. If the driver of the SUV hadn't slammed on his brakes, Avery would be dead.

Allie stood behind her mother, staring at Avery. "Is she going to be all right?"

"Yes," Tara said. "It'll take some time. She'll need your help."

"What about her face?"

"We'll do plastic surgery. You'll hardly notice."

"Mom?"

"What is it?"

"I'm glad it wasn't me."

"That's okay, baby."

Tara's phone buzzed and after checking to see who it was, she left the room and was gone for twenty minutes.

Allie fell asleep in a chair. When Tara returned, she motioned Neal into the hall. Since the morning, she'd aged. New lines appeared beneath her eyes. She'd run her fingers through her hair so often it looked slept on. "While you were in X-ray, I talked to Avery's psychologist. He said we should be prepared for her learning disabilities to worsen. She's going to need a lot of extra support."

A responsible father would make sure Avery got what she needed. Especially after causing the accident. Neal had once been that man but wasn't any longer. "BMW will pay for it. The side airbag never opened." He'd already decided a lawyer would jump at the case.

"What happened, anyway?" she asked.

Bright light bounced off the walls and the linoleum floor. It seemed an appropriate place for an interrogation. "We were arguing and I didn't see the red light."

"Arguing about what?"

Neal hesitated, but Avery was bound to tell Tara. She might as well hear it from him. "Cash she found in the car. She wanted to keep it."

Tara had rushed to the hospital from work and still wore her tailored gray suit and narrow pumps. She leaned against the wall, uncomfortable in the shoes or the conversation, or both. "How much was it?" she asked.

"A lot."

She wrapped her arms around her chest. "You're planning to leave us."

"You're the one having an affair."

"We just talk."

There was pain in her voice, but Neal couldn't help noticing her use of the present tense. "You never meet in person?"

Carrying a stack of clean sheets, a nurse's aide glided by.

"What if we do?"

"That's what I thought."

Neal spent the next day in the hospital with Avery, who had been given Tramadol and slept most of the time. When she was awake, she refused to speak to him unless she wanted something. In the hospital gift shop, he bought the copies of *Elle* and *Vogue* she asked for.

"I'll never look this good. Not anymore," she said, when he handed them over, her speech a beat slower than usual. A few minutes later, she closed her eyes, and the magazines slipped to the floor.

"My life is over," she said when she woke up. "I hope you're happy." There was nothing he could say that wouldn't make her angrier. She told him to get her a Diet Coke and a salad. "Not from the cafeteria. From the deli on Lakeville."

He doubted she'd have the appetite for it but was glad for the break. He walked to the store. Before he went in, he called Felicia. "If the airbag had deployed, she wouldn't have been injured," he said.

"Bad things happen. She'll be all right."

"You think so?"

"Yes. You want to come by?"

"Not now."

He returned with Avery's lunch. About to enter the room, he heard her sobbing. If he went in, she'd stop, so he sank to his heels and waited.

"It's about time," she said, when he brought in the food, her voice quiet. "You took forever." Neal gathered crumpled tissues from the bed, dropped them into the trash. The food sat on the bedside tray, untouched.

Tara arrived after work, and Neal left, driving her Buick, stopping at home to pack a suitcase before heading to the pizza shop. Tara would find someone to replace him, perhaps already had.

A time would come when he would regret leaving while Avery was still in the hospital, when he would ache for his girls, whom he still loved, and when he would question abandoning Tara despite what she had done. But for now, Neal felt only relief.

Mama Jane kneaded dough without looking at it, pressing it and folding it over itself. The dough looked pure and smelled ripe with yeast. Neal briefly wished he were a pizza chef instead of a delivery guy, but then realized he'd be stuck in the tiny overheated store.

Neal delivered to a regular who asked how he was and to several new customers, all of it uncomplicated and pleasant. He didn't even mind the Buick. It would turn into a beater, cracks in the windshield he couldn't afford to fix, stains in the carpet, and half a dozen mysterious dents. Used pieces of gum would continue to roll around the floor, pelting Neal's shoes and reminding him of the family he'd once had, until the last one disappeared in a seat's floor track, and they were gone.

Couch

~~~~~~~~~~
~~~~~~

It was a strange couch for a therapist's office. It was so tall, a grown
man sitting on it felt like a child, his feet dangling inches from
the floor. The cushion was so soft, it swallowed large women, pro-
longing their stay. Though covered in raw silk, the seams were frayed
and revealed crumbling foam. Penelope would not have chosen such
a couch, but she had inherited it from her grandmother just as she
was starting her practice twenty years before on a shoestring bud-
get. Over the years, though the couch deteriorated and her practice
grew, she couldn't bring herself to replace it. Without quite realiz-
ing it, Penelope had come to believe the couch was responsible for
her success. So she ignored the cracks in the legs, the way the frame
creaked, telling herself it had many more good seasons.

At two o'clock, Penelope stuck her head into the waiting room
and greeted Estelle Markowitz. The elderly woman had lost her husband, a man she hadn't cared for and whom she had spent forty
years berating. Rocking on the couch, Estelle wept because she

missed her husband and because she had wasted her life with someone who picked his teeth until he had none left to pick. Then he switched to adjusting his dentures, a habit Estelle found even more repulsive. She told all this to Penelope, who clucked and nodded and said, "What a terrible shame" and "I'm so sorry." Thinking about her own failed marriage, Penelope let out a deep sigh that startled her client.

Penelope sat across from Estelle in a swivel chair that allowed her to reach for the tissues on her desk and roll to the couch all in one continuous motion. Although Penelope never would have admitted it, and was hardly aware of it herself, she enjoyed rolling around the office, even if it was to deliver tissues to a client who was crying. She was a short, heavy woman, and rolling made her feel light. She allowed the client a single tissue, never surrendering the box, so she might have an excuse to swivel and roll several times during the session.

The couch caught a number of Estelle Markowitz's tears, just as earlier in the day it had absorbed Jack Green's, and the day before, Roger Barber's. Over two decades, so many tears had landed on the couch, the cushion was shot through with salt. In the summer, patients experienced a mysterious burning sensation on the backs of their exposed legs, but at one hundred and eighty dollars an hour, it didn't seem worth mentioning.

When her fifty minutes were up, Estelle shoved the soggy tissues into her purse and wrote out a check.

"Same time next week?" Penelope asked.

"Yes," Estelle answered, because she still felt like crying. Estelle Markowitz had been riding the bus from her Upper West Side apartment to Penelope's office every Tuesday afternoon for two years, but it was as if her husband had died yesterday. She had a difficult time climbing off the couch. She felt for a moment—although she knew it was ridiculous—that the couch was restraining her. When she finally freed herself, she heard a loud groan as the worn-out frame contracted.

"Everything all right?" Penelope asked.

Estelle wondered briefly whether Penelope was addressing the couch. "I had a bit of trouble getting my footing."

"You're not dizzy, are you? Perhaps you'd like to sit in the waiting room until it passes." The chairs in the waiting room were from an office supply store and to Penelope's knowledge had never given her clients any trouble.

At three o'clock, Penelope met with Tara, whose boyfriend, Axel, had infected her with herpes before dumping her for her best friend. Tara touched her tongue ring to her lip and related all the nasty things Axel said about her. Only half were true, she assured Penelope. Picking at the bandages on her wrists, Tara said she couldn't live without Axel.

"Tell me about your childhood," Penelope said, thinking about her own past and the heartbreak she experienced each time her father chose her delicate sister to ride in the truck with him as he delivered cartons of Pepsi to soda shops on Long Island. Penelope dabbed her eyes. Then she rolled to Tara and offered her a tissue, but the young woman preferred to wipe her leaking nose on the sleeve of her black spandex shirt, which was no fun for Penelope. Large tears splattered the couch, and the girl tried to wipe those with her sleeve, too. It was Tara's third session, and Penelope had the feeling she'd be coming for a while.

After Tara left, Penelope opened the door to her office closet and stared at the gym bag she'd packed ten weeks before. She hadn't scheduled a four o'clock so she could beat the after-work rush at the health club. She'd never experienced the rush, but she could imagine it: svelte twentysomethings in leotards pedaling to earsplitting hip-hop. Designer breasts to match their designer running shoes. Penelope hadn't been to the club at all since she signed up at the end of a tour given by a half-naked body builder, who complimented her eyes and touched her lightly on the back while handing her a pen. She grabbed her coat and shut the closet door before the bag could escape, leaping into her hand and dragging her off to the place.

On the front of the door, a dog leash hung from a metal hook. Its leather was worn and cracked, chewed in one spot from the time she had tied Jung outside a coffee shop and lingered over the crossword. As Penelope massaged the rough strap between her fingers, she pictured the dog's charcoal muzzle and brown eyes.

She went to Murphy's, where the bartender poured a double Scotch without her having to ask. He was young and handsome, with red hair and blue eyes, and he made Penelope feel old. She didn't know why she kept coming back. It was a place she had come with her ex-husband, one of the few things Dion surrendered in a bitter divorce. She often imagined Dion's face reflected in beer steins waitresses carried to off-duty cops who huddled in antique oak booths.

Before the divorce, Penelope would rush home after work to take their German shepherds out. Freud and Jung would drag her through Central Park, peeing on every leaf and branch, sniffing the Great Dane in a studded collar and the bichon frise who needed a haircut, sniffing their owners, too. Penelope wrenched a creased picture of the dogs from her wallet and laid it on the bar.

Penelope still had a key to the apartment she and Dion had

shared. She would stop by in the middle of the day sometimes, check his e-mail, and rifle his drawers. From cloudy Tupperware, she would feed Freud leftovers, spooning just enough onto his plate that Dion wouldn't notice anything missing but might finish dinner a bit hungry. The judge's final order had given Freud to Dion and Jung to Penelope, but only a month later, Jung had been diagnosed with cancer. He had lived another six months. Penelope knew she should get another dog—the ASPCA was crowded and her heart was empty—but even five years after the divorce, she couldn't imagine replacing either dog.

Halfway through a session the next morning, the couch collapsed. The silk ripped down the middle, the cushion crumpled, and the frame snapped in two, each half pressing onto a trembling Brian Walston who, as it happened, was describing a dream in which the walls were caving in. Penelope didn't know what to say. None of her standard responses seemed appropriate—not "Of course you feel that way," or "It's okay to feel sad," or even "That must have hurt you," though that was by far the closest. When she regained her composure, she rose from her chair and helped Brian up. She fed him a muscle relaxant from the stash in her purse, rescheduled his session, and set off to find a new couch.

She tried Macy's first. If she had been looking for a leather couch, she could have had her pick in orange or topaz or gray. She had to restrain her impulse to pinch the floor manager's fleshy arm when he persisted in steering her from one modern couch to another, since—hadn't she told him?—she wanted something traditional. But when he showed her fabric couches in neutral tones, she hated them. The showroom's fluorescent lighting tired her eyes. No matter where she looked, the view was the same: row after row of empty living rooms, cardboard books and television sets masquerading as the real thing, and a salesman whose comb-over told her everything she needed to know—he lived alone and ate TV dinners.

The problem, Penelope admitted to herself over a double latte and a plate of Italian cookies, was that she wasn't keen on a new couch at all. She wanted her grandmother's couch. But it was beyond repair.

She spent the afternoon hunting through SoHo boutiques filled with furniture from the 1960s and '70s. She sat on a black leather couch, its cushion no thicker than a slice of pizza, its chrome frame reflecting the dark lines that stretched across her brow. She ran her hand over a wavy plastic couch but couldn't picture it in her office. Tears would pool on the surface.

She had all but given up when she entered a secondhand store on Fifth Street in the East Village. Framed pictures of poodles and greyhounds decorated the shop walls. And then Penelope saw it: rattan frame stained deep brown, brocade cushions the color of sea foam. From one of the cushions, she removed a Tiffany lamp. She stood up a statue of Saint Paul that rested against the arm. Trying to walk around the couch, she ran into a rolltop desk and a dinette. When she sat on the couch, she discovered the seats were firm, and her feet fell squarely on the dusty plywood floor. Though minutes before she had been exhausted from traipsing all over town, suddenly she felt refreshed. She gazed at the cushions, taken with how sunlight streaming through the store window—sunlight that should have been blocked by the townhouse across the street—glanced off the fabric.

"Hello?" she called. Although the door was open, no one seemed to be minding the store. "Anybody here?" From the scratched glass counter, she took one of the store's cards, its edges perforated and imperfectly torn. "Hello!" she cried out, louder this time, but no one emerged. Frustrated, she kicked Saint Paul, leaving a dent in his robes.

When she returned the next day, the door was open again, but as before, no one was there. She was surprised they didn't worry about theft. She left a note on the counter, asking someone to call her. Although she gave the numbers for her home, office, and cell phone, she didn't hear from anyone.

For the remainder of the week, her patients sat on a folding chair she brought from home. They squirmed. Their bottoms grew sore, their tempers short. No one felt comfortable enough to cry, and wasn't the very point of coming to a therapist's office to weep without apology? Several clients cancelled sessions, claiming to be ill or too busy.

The third time Penelope visited the store, a woman whose white hair was tied in a neat chignon greeted her. The shopkeeper wore Lee overalls and was dusting the old-fashioned cash register. Penelope was so relieved to find someone there, she got right to the point. "How much is the couch?"

The woman looked hard at Penelope and then at the couch. She shook her head. "I'm afraid it's not for sale. Perhaps I can interest you in some antique coins or a first-edition Hemingway?" Using the sleeve of her cotton shirt to remove fingerprints from a crystal vase, the shopkeeper resumed her cleaning.

"What do you mean it's not for sale? It's right in the middle of the store." It was all Penelope could do to keep from stomping her foot.

The woman set down the vase. "You are very observant. You will note the statue of Saint Paul is also in the middle of the store. So if it is something in the middle of the store you want, surely the statue will do. Think how much easier it will be to transport."

Penelope approached the shopkeeper. "I don't want a statue or a book or antique coins. I need a couch for my office, and I want this one."

"Yes, I can see you want it. But we don't always get what we want, now do we?" The woman began unpacking a large box of books, lining them on a shelf Penelope could have sworn had been full a moment before.

If Penelope hadn't desired the sofa so badly, she would have broken something, perhaps the Tiffany lamp, and if they had met under different circumstances, she would have given the shopkeeper her card, as the woman was clearly suffering from some sort of mental disease. Instead, Penelope said, "Why would you have it out if you're not going to sell it?"

"As to selling it, well, I had intended to, but then you arrived, and if I'm not mistaken, the couch got a little sad. It seemed to lose a bit of its sparkle." The woman set a book on top of the box and turned back toward Penelope. "Let's be honest. You make people cry."

A chill went through Penelope. "How do you know—"

"Oh, let's not worry about that."

Penelope struggled to stay calm; she remembered leaving her contact information the last time she had been at the store and figured the woman had looked her up. "I don't make people cry. I let them cry. There's a difference."

"Is there?"

Penelope clutched the back of a pine rocker. There was no point fighting with the woman, who obviously didn't understand how therapy worked. "I lost my grandmother's couch. I've looked all over the city for a suitable replacement, and this is the only one I've found."

The shopkeeper rested her hand on the back of the couch. "Have you tried Macy's?"

Groaning, Penelope leaned against the rocker.

"If you don't mind, that's an antique." The woman sighed. She patted the top of the couch. "I'm not an unreasonable woman. And I've a fondness for grandmothers, myself. Perhaps I've been too hasty."

Penelope slid her checkbook from her purse.

"It will not be an easy couch for you," the shopkeeper said. "Are you sure you wouldn't rather have Saint Paul?"

"I'm sure. How much is it?"

"In honor of your grandmother, you may have it. Perhaps you will make a contribution to the ASPCA."

Penelope wondered if the shopkeeper, too, had lost a dog.

<hr>

When Estelle Markowitz first saw the couch, she regarded it with suspicion, poking the cushions and trying not to be obvious about sniffing the fabric. But once she sat on it, she realized it was a definite improvement. The couch supported her back, and her feet rested comfortably on the carpet. She told Penelope she was thinking about going to the senior center to play mah-jongg, which she had enjoyed when she was young. And she said she might fly to California to see her youngest son's new house. She didn't know where these ideas had come from. All morning she had been stewing about the way her husband used to complain whenever she bought a hat. *He begrudged me my one pleasure in life—hats!* she had planned to tell Penelope. But now she was so pleased with everything she had to look forward to, she forgot to complain. She didn't cry once. Not even when she talked about her dead husband, Sol. "He couldn't help losing his teeth," she said. "And he only played with his dentures because they weren't a good fit. He wasn't a cruel man." At the end of the session, Estelle told Penelope, "I'm feeling so much better. I don't think I'll need any more appointments."

Penelope didn't know what to say.

When Tara came for her appointment, she told Penelope about Jackson, a boy she had met at the health clinic. Jackson had herpes, too. But when Axel found out she was seeing someone else, he came to her house with a bag of pot. Axel said they were both tainted, so what the hell, and mounted her on the coffee table. "You know," Tara said, getting comfortable on the new couch, "Axel is a dickwad. I think I'll call Jackson." She told Penelope about the way Jackson stuck his head out of the window of the city bus and shouted, "Peace, Miss Tara!" and held up two fingers until she couldn't see him anymore. She said she liked kissing him even though he had braces. "They're the soft plastic kind, and he never has food stuck in them." Then she hopped off the couch and left the session ten minutes early.

Although Penelope waited, poised with a full box of tissues, not a drop of moisture fell onto the new couch. Over the next few weeks, Jack Green, Roger Barber, and Brian Walston all discovered brighter outlooks and quit therapy. For the first time in Penelope's career, her practice began to dwindle. She had to dip into her savings to pay her office rent, and some days there was no reason to go into the office at all. She blamed the new couch and decided to return it. But the store's business card didn't list a phone number, and when she made a trip to the East Village to arrange to have the couch picked up, the shop had vanished. She hired two college students to put it out on the curb. Though the men who had delivered it didn't have any trouble bringing it in, the students couldn't seem to fit it through the door.

Penelope spent more and more time at Murphy's. After several drinks, she would lean over the bar, cursing her father and Dion. The next morning she would wake up with a swollen tongue and little memory of when or how she had made it home.

Six months had passed since Penelope acquired the new couch. Her appointment book empty, she lay around her apartment in sweats, newspaper spread out before her. She read the same sentence over and over, something about a water main break on Bleecker Street or a break-in on Water Street. Finally, she gave up and attempted to wash dishes that had sat in the sink for a week, hardened food particles clinging like an industrial epoxy to the flatware. Her apartment hadn't been cleaned in months. Walking from the kitchen to her bedroom, she stepped onto detritus from two seasons: crushed autumn leaves and crystals of SnoMelt. Despite paying an exorbitant rent, she felt she had somehow ended up on the street.

Later that day, she visited Dion's apartment. As soon as she inserted the key into the lock, Freud began to whine, and he nearly knocked her over when she stepped inside. Penelope buried her nose in his neck, inhaling a soup of fur and dust. She rubbed his ears, scratched his back, and played patty-cake on his belly. She fed him treats, delighting in his thick drool and the thumping of his heavy tail on the carpet. They spent the better part of the afternoon napping on the floor.

The next day, she had a ten o'clock, a referral from Estelle Markowitz. In the past, Penelope had looked forward to meeting a new patient, to commiserating as the patient related a tragic story. She had little to look forward to anymore. Patients so depressed they questioned the value of their lives, so anxious they rarely left their homes, found relief as soon as they settled onto the sea-foam cushions.

That's how it went with the new client. Penelope doubted she would see him again. When he left, though it was still morning, tiredness overcame her. Her limbs felt like damp wood; her breath came in shallow huffs. She pulled herself from her chair, lay on the new couch, and fell into a heavy sleep. Awaking revitalized an hour later, she discovered the newspaper open to the classifieds on her desk, though she was sure she'd last been reading the obits.

She called to place an ad in the services section, promising quick results. The following morning, she joined the chamber of commerce and attended two meetings, handing out business cards. Over the next month, she had a website built that featured the new couch on the home page. People whose unhappiness had thrummed below the surface for years happened onto the site and felt a deep longing. As fast as she could open their e-mails, new ones filled her in-box, each message a plea for her first available appointment.

She no longer spent sessions saying "How awful" and "I'm so sorry" as she encouraged clients to examine their pasts. Instead, she had clients draw up "happiness blueprints." She cried, "Try it!" and "Why not?" She began to view each patient's unhappiness as a puzzle, and as she searched for solutions, she briefly forgot her own problems. The box of tissues was relegated to the closet. But the greater help she was to clients, the sooner they left her. Her practice was like a train station, with strangers always passing through.

Anticipating a visit to Murphy's one afternoon, she went to retrieve her coat from the office closet. The next thing she knew, she was heading to the health club, the gym bag pulling her along. It didn't surprise her to run into Estelle Markowitz training on cardio circuit.

After meeting with three new clients the following morning, she stretched out on the couch with a copy of *Techniques in Short-Term Therapy*. She had read only a few sentences before she became impatient. Signs of spring filtered through the open window. Central Park was lovely on such days, light glinting off the duck pond, city dwellers sprawled out on blankets, greedily consuming novels and sunshine.

She squeezed the key to Dion's apartment, considering how much Freud would enjoy a romp through the park. It had been weeks since she'd run her fingers through his ruff. She wondered what Dion was up to, whether he'd met anyone.

The sound of a dog barking, high, sharp calls aimed at her office, startled her; the key slipped from her fingers. She hurried to the window, but the only dog she saw—a German shepherd, as it happened—was walking quietly alongside its owner. She turned back for the key, but it wasn't on the couch. Lifting each cushion and then removing them all, she didn't find it. It wasn't on the floor, either. Kneeling to peer beneath the rattan frame, she discovered only dust. She emptied her purse onto the carpet, thinking perhaps it had fallen back inside. But the key was gone. The damn couch had swallowed it.

Sitting on the floor, she picked up a dried-out mascara brush and two sticky pennies from the carpet and dropped them back into her purse. A pen sporting her new motto, "Brief is better," had rolled under her chair. Reaching for it, she pinched her finger under a caster.

She cursed the chair and sucked on the bruise. In front of the couch lay her wallet. The photo of Freud and Jung stuck out between two bills.

She had lost Dion and Jung, and now without the key, she would lose Freud, too. She wept, her breath coming in coarse gasps, her vision clouding. As she groped the top of her desk for tissues, she remembered they were no longer there.

Finally, she stopped. Sounds—the bang and scrape of metal as one car after another hit the pothole in front of her office, the rustle of a pigeon's wings when it took off from the ledge, the blaring of horns—entered her office, reminding her of a world outside herself. She began to put the room in order. Seeing Jung's leash on its hook, she remembered all at once the shopkeeper's suggestion that she contribute to the ASPCA. Best not to cross the odd woman, Penelope decided.

The shelter wasn't far from her office, the brisk walk taking her past the Park Avenue tulips. It seemed to Penelope their colors had grown sharper, their edges more defined, since she had last seen them. When she arrived at the shelter, she was out of breath. She planned to avoid the kennels. Not ready to adopt a new dog, she didn't want to be tempted. She would never be able to replace Freud or Jung, and even if a dog did manage to capture her heart, it, too, would die one day, leaving her alone. She told herself she would just make a donation and leave. But first, she needed to rest. In the corner of the lobby, she noticed an old sofa and headed toward it. Its well-worn cushions lay helter-skelter on an oak frame, and its back was elaborately carved with lions and wolves. It was a strange couch for a shelter.

Yiddish Lessons

~~~~~~~~~~
~~~~~~~

A tragedy. A child who had just learned to walk, to say father, *tati,* that child died. An unnecessary death. A fall. Because someone left a window open and looked away.

~~~~~~~~

My aunt Leah wore a blond wig. The other Crown Heights women wore black or brown wigs, styled close to the head, but Leah wore a movie star's wig, long and loose. I thought she was beautiful. She was pale, and her fingers were slender. Her nose, which others might have considered sharp, I regarded as regal.

When I was growing up, I would sometimes mop her kitchen floor. She seemed too delicate to do it herself. Though I was only eleven and her brother's daughter, she didn't stop me.

"Mameleh," she'd say, "bring the roast up from the basement," and I'd go down to the freezer and lug the icy slab up the stairs. My hands ached from the cold, but I would have endured

worse for the smile she gave me as I passed her on the way to the sink.

My own mother was nothing like her. Short and heavy, my mother wore her hair in a bun and covered it only when she went to synagogue. Leah wore dresses that belted at her diminutive waist, lively prints that fell like petals around her. My mother wore black pants two sizes too small, her belly protruding like a cartoon bomb, only the glowing fuse missing.

I was deaf to my mother's requests for help. "Vacuum the rug," she would plead Friday afternoon as the sun lowered and the Sabbath approached. A mere ten-by-ten square of carpet, but I wouldn't do it. "Please, it's almost *Shabbos*." I would pretend I hadn't heard, lying facedown on my unmade bed, reading *Little Women*. What did she have to bargain with? Kisses? I took her kisses for granted because they were as plentiful as the water that flowed from the tap.

As beautiful as Leah was, her husband was that unattractive. With his great round face and wispy hairs growing from his chin, he resembled a boar. He would stuff an apple into his mouth and devour it, stem, core, and all. He never simply said my aunt's name but instead bellowed it in an unrecognizable accent.

I could tell Leah had contempt for him. Although her own clothes were immaculate, she let his go for weeks without washing, grime building up around his shirt collar until it was as dark as charcoal. They had two children, a boy and a girl. The girl, Bruriah, looked like her father with fat cheeks and so many small, dark freckles it was as if someone had sprinkled her face with pepper. Whenever the ten-year-old approached, my aunt remembered an errand she had to run or that it was time to punch down the dough. With her fifteen-year-old son, Yankel, it was different. It didn't matter that he, too, had a moon-shaped face. She adored him and would go so far as to interrupt her prayers when he entered a room.

Each day after school, while my mother answered phones in my father's textile factory, I visited my aunt. Her children were off in their bedrooms, Yankel doing schoolwork and Bruriah drawing pictures of broken birds and dead flowers. I sat in the kitchen with Leah and bragged about my test scores and how I'd survived a game of dodgeball. She buttered thick slices of rye bread for me and served them with tea in a glass. I was built like my mother and got plenty to eat at home, but the food was a gift from her, so I devoured it, growing hungrier with each bite.

She began to teach me Yiddish, writing out sentences in lined blue booklets. *Der feter iz fet.* The uncle is fat.

Once, during a lesson, Bruriah ventured halfway into the kitchen, the toes of her scuffed Mary Janes on the linoleum, her heels on the hall carpet. She rocked back and forth, glancing at the half-eaten loaf on the table. "Can I have some, too?" Her voice was full of sorrow, her face swollen with dejection, anticipating the refusal she must have known would come, for even I knew, and I was just a guest.

"You're hungry?" My aunt continued to write.

"Yes, Mama."

"Have an apple."

"How come she gets it?"

Leah's head snapped up. "Don't call your cousin *she*. It's not polite."

"How come Rivkah gets it?"

"You had enough to eat today. Leave us alone."

"*Di tokhter iz fet.*" The daughter is fat, she said to me when Bruriah was gone, and we both laughed.

Naturally, everything changed the instant Yankel came into the kitchen. He was above noticing me.

"*Tateleh,* what can I get you?" she asked. "Rivkah, pour him some tea. You want a slice of pie? Rivkah, not the old pie, the fresh one." I handed her the pie tin, and she placed it on the blue booklet, staining the paper with grease.

He sat down next to her, and she caressed his ruddy cheeks with her fingertips. I purposely forgot the sugar, but she jumped up to get it and dropped three lumps in the glass, one at a time, making sure the water didn't splatter. She stirred it for him and rested the spoon on a plate.

I watched from a corner as they whispered to each other. No one invited me to sit down, so I went home.

Entering my house, I slammed the door behind me. My mother was in the kitchen preparing dinner. "What is it?" she said.

"Nothing."

"You want a snack?" A worn terry-cloth apron was tied around her waist.

"I'm not hungry."

"I'm making minute steaks for dinner." With the back of her hand, she pushed a loose strand of hair from her eyes, her fingers still holding the garlic she had been rubbing into the meat.

"I said I wasn't hungry."

"Wait till you see them." She was eternally optimistic, and since I loved to eat, she wasn't disappointed. That night, as my parents talked over the day's business, trading words like *orders* and *shipments*, *returns* and *remainders*, I sliced through the steak, imagining I was cutting Yankel's hand away from a sweetened glass of tea.

My father was as handsome as his sister Leah was delicate, with reddish hair and high cheekbones. He wore three-piece suits even on the weekends. His only concession to leisure was to leave the vest unbuttoned. When he wasn't working, he was in his study, a somber room crowded with ancient texts that lined the walls and sat in piles on his desk. He spent hours in his high-backed chair, hovering over tall volumes of Torah and Talmud.

I had asked him to teach me the sacred wisdom, but he said it was forbidden for girls to pronounce the holy words. "If I had a son it would be different." He shook his head and went back to his studies, ignoring me although I lingered alongside his desk.

When my father was at work, I sometimes took the books down, their cracked leather bindings crumbling in my hands. I stared at the long pages, groups of words arranged around central texts, their meanings hidden from me. I didn't dare sit in my father's seat and instead settled cross-legged on the floor, inhaling the smell of disintegrating glue. Once, I took a fountain pen from my father's desk and blotted out the name of God.

"There is only mourning when a girl enters the world," I had overheard my father say, commiserating with a neighbor whose wife had just given birth. For years, I wondered why a girl should be deprived of afternoon or evening, but from my father's tone I knew he was describing a tragedy, like the dropping of a holy scroll or the accidental ingestion of pork.

My mother was constantly pregnant, but a dybbuk inhabited her womb, and she was unable to carry another child to term. She prayed endlessly to relieve her condition, bowing and beating her breast in the synagogue, while I stood next to her, bored and counting the pages to the conclusion of the service. In the end, my parents were left with only me.

I cut my hair short and wore boy's clothes. I peed standing up, using a plastic funnel I found in the kitchen to direct the yellow stream. One day my mother brought me a gift, a bomber jacket from the Army Navy store, a strip of tape advertising the size—boy's medium—stuck prominently on the chest. I put it on and ran into my father's study. Did I hope to deceive him, as Jacob had deceived Isaac? I should have known his eyesight was too good for that.

"It's forbidden!" he shouted, wagging his finger at my mother, who was standing in the doorway. "The girl mustn't masquerade as a boy!" He flew from his seat and grabbed the jacket by the collar. With an upward motion he yanked it off, twisting my arms and lifting me to my toes. He shook it in my face. The polyester fibers gave off melancholy vibrations as the sleeves rubbed against the body of the jacket. He took it out to his car, and I never saw it again.

Leah continued with our lessons, reciting vocabulary while I peeled potatoes for the *cholent*, the beef and bean stew she served for Sabbath lunch. "*Meydl*, girl, *eyfele*, baby, *yingl*, boy, like my Yankel, oy, what a boy, a mother couldn't ask for more. Such a smart boy, such a good boy, such respect he shows his mother. You'll be lucky to have such a boy. Look at your poor mother what she goes through."

In the middle of this speech, I cut myself with the peeler. I let the blood flow over the potatoes and dropped them into the pot.

~~~~~~~~~~

Over the next few years, my father's factory prospered, but wealth failed to bring him happiness. Yankel graduated from high school and went off to rabbinical school in Baltimore. While my classmates helped their mothers, pushing younger siblings in strollers and learning to bake *challah*, my aunt and I chatted away in Yiddish. Bruriah had refused to speak since she turned twelve, so there was no one to interrupt us. Once, sitting across the kitchen table from me, Leah grabbed my hand and brought it to her chest, and I knew I was the daughter she had always wanted.

Yankel returned home one weekend each month. Days before his arrival, my aunt began preparing. By Thursday afternoon, she was elbow deep in *kugel,* stirring the glutinous mass of noodles, eggs, raisins, and sugar. She fried batches of *kichelkies,* sprinkling the puffed-up cookies with confectioner's sugar after they cooled. She scoured the house, wiping dust from the tops of door moldings and airing out coverlets on the clothesline in the backyard. She inventoried the refrigerator and tossed aging food to the neighborhood cat. Even as I helped her stuff veal roasts and wax floors, I prayed for a great train wreck on Amtrak's Baltimore–New York line.

One Sabbath my uncle began discussing marriage possibilities for Yankel. Sitting at our dining-room table, he asked my father about this family and that one. I hoped Yankel would find a foreign girl, one from London or at least New Jersey. When she heard the word *marriage,* my aunt choked on a lump of gefilte fish, her eyes watering. She was sitting next to Yankel and when her airways finally cleared, she clutched the sleeve of his suit jacket and wouldn't let go.

"What about Malkah Bina, the butcher's daughter?" my cousin Bruriah rasped. "They could have *flanken* every night."

"No one asked you," my aunt said, and with that, Bruriah retired her vocal cords for another half dozen years, until she finally escaped to live a bohemian life in Prague.

"A rabbi can always make a good match," my father said, twisting a fine lace napkin that had come from his factory. He looked at me. A girl of fifteen, I no longer fit into boy's clothes. Overnight, my body had become a swollen curve, my face a mass of angry red hormones. The lace ripped. My father laid the torn napkin on his lap and sighed. "You're a lucky man."

"What is luck?" my uncle said, leaning back in his chair and raising his hands to the heavens, "but a blessing from the Almighty."

Yankel pried his mother's fingers from his jacket. "God said in Genesis, 'It is not good for a man to be alone. I will make a helper for him.'"

"You're too young for a helper," Leah said.

"But I'm not, Mama." He scratched his scalp, pulled on his earlobes, and smoothed his pants, only to begin again, scratch, pull, smooth. His face glimmered with sweat.

At first it was just talk, but eventually parents brought their daughters to meet Yankel. I was not invited to these meetings, but I heard about the girls from my aunt.

"Her teeth were like planks. The family must be poor or they would have fixed them—sawed them down, moved them back, something. And when she sipped her tea, what a noise. Loud as a lawn mower. Someone played hooky from charm school." And about another: "I grant you, this one was pretty. But what kind of a name is Janice? Her skirt was so short, I caught a glimpse of you-know-what. She's studying accounting. Just what my Yankel needs, a girl smarter than he is. I can hear it already, 'No, Yankel, this way. Not that way, Yankel. How hard is it to understand, Yankel?' Better a stupid girl who won't make him feel small."

She began to discourage Yankel from coming home. I heard her on the phone. "Are you sure you don't need to study? It's such a long train ride. Stay for the weekend. Eat dinner at the rabbi's. They'd be happy to have you. The rabbi's wife assured me, she said, 'Any time

Yankel wants to stay, he's welcome at our house for *Shabbos*.' You don't want to insult them."

He stayed at school until my uncle became suspicious. "Where's Yankel?" he demanded one Friday afternoon when it became apparent Leah wasn't setting off for the train station. "I've got three girls for him to meet, and he's never home. Doesn't he want to see his parents? Leah!"

"I'll tell him you want to see him."

My uncle pulled at the hairs on his chin. I held my breath, afraid he would tear out a chunk of flesh. "Just tell him to come home!" he said.

The parade of girls resumed, and I noticed a change in my aunt. Her wig, which had once sat so perfectly, tilted to one side, revealing strands of her silver-gray hair. A snag appeared in her stockings, a mere pull at first, the nylon thread hanging like a bride's train. Over time, the snag blossomed into a run and then a tear, revealing yellow flesh and purple veins.

I tried everything to get her attention. I ridiculed her daughter Bruriah's isolation and her husband's ripe odor. My aunt gave me a weak smile, but it smacked of pity and only served to infuriate me. I translated famous speeches—the "Gettysburg Address" and "I Have a Dream"—into Yiddish and performed them for her in her kitchen, but I couldn't tell if she heard. She stopped cleaning. Mildew coated the bathroom walls. Dust settled onto the surface of the matzo-ball soup, which remained on the stove for days. When I offered to clean, she ignored me.

Yankel got engaged. The girl's name was Tamar, and she was finely proportioned, with hair the color of almond shells and large green eyes. Her lips were always lightly parted and moved easily into a smile. She never spoke of herself. Unable to find fault with her, my aunt became mute, her mouth shrinking like a raisin. Tamar's father was a successful diamond cutter with workshops in New York and Jerusalem.

Yankel came home every weekend to see her. He trimmed his beard and changed his shirt morning and evening. He began carrying breath freshener and a comb. I never saw him pass a mirror without stopping to inspect himself, to remove the food particles migrating through his beard, and to curl the side locks that hung to his shoulders. He was deaf to all but Tamar's voice and let the tea his mother poured grow cold.

Leah didn't give up. She prepared his favorite foods and sprinkled lavender oil on his bedsheets. She purchased herbs from the Levite witch, whose potions were said to win back straying lovers. She mixed them in with the *cholent* and served him an extra large portion. Bloated and farting, Yankel stayed by Tamar's side.

The marriage was celebrated for seven nights. Each night the caterer served seven courses, never repeating a dish. A klezmer band played, the fiddle drawing guests onto the dance floor where they squatted and kicked out their legs in a vigorous *kezatzke* and hoisted the bride and groom in their seats. Yankel's eyes lingered on his bride's face. He spoke softly to her, not as his father spoke to his mother, but as his mother spoke to him, asking after her every need, though it wasn't the custom for men to wait on their wives.

After the wedding, the couple moved into an apartment in Baltimore, so Yankel could complete his studies. When they visited Crown Heights, they stayed with Tamar's parents, whose house was spacious and cleaned by servants.

"Is the meat more tender there? The fruit sweeter?" Leah asked no one in particular. She banged a ladle on the counter, splattering hot liquid across the room.

One day, she took out a fresh blue book and began to write. She composed a poem about the angel of death. I memorized the verses and recited it back to her the next day. "You're my only friend," she said, resting her head on the table.

I brought her roses I cut from a neighbor's bush. Deprived of water, they wilted. When she served me pie, I cut away the mold and made grateful noises as I ate the rest. What did I care if she wrapped her hair in an old kerchief and allowed her stockings to bunch around her ankles? She said barely a word when we were together. Her body limp, her eyes closed, I worried she might fall from her chair. I talked enough for both of us, content to be in the same room with her.

⁓⁓⁓⁓⁓

One year after the wedding, Tamar gave birth to a baby boy. So perfect was the child in his parents' eyes, they were convinced his birth was a miracle, and they hung five-fingered *hamsas* in every corner of their apartment to ward off evil spirits. Tamar's father invited half of Brooklyn to the bris. Buffet tables spilled over with delicacies, herring swimming in cream sauce, entire schools of smoked whitefish, black eyes staring out of oily faces. Fat bagels were trucked in from Manhattan by the gross. New Jersey tomato farms were denuded for the occasion.

My father wore his best wool suit, the one he wore to synagogue on the High Holy Days. When Yankel passed him the baby, my father cradled the boy to his chest and kissed his hair. I snuck my hand under the child's blanket and pinched his eight-day-old thigh hard enough to bruise it. His face screwed up with pain. "He must have gas," I said. The ceremony was about to start, but my father wouldn't give up the child. It took three men to pry him from my father's arms.

A few weeks after the bris, Leah straightened her wig and went to stay with the new parents in Baltimore. She was gone for a week. When she returned, all she talked about was the baby. "I was changing his diaper and all of a sudden, he made such a fountain. I laughed so hard tears ran down my cheeks. And when he saw me laughing, he started laughing, too. Did you ever hear of such a thing? Such a smart baby!"

I recited the Pledge of Allegiance in my head as she talked. "My class is going on a trip to Washington. We're touring the White House and the Senate."

"Why Tamar has to use cloth diapers, I don't know. What's wrong with plastic? The cloth ones give him rashes. I tried to tell her, but she looks at me like I'm some old lady."

I hummed "My Country, 'Tis of Thee." Then I said, "We're seeing the Smithsonian and the Air and Space Museum."

"He looks just like my Yankel looked. Oy. I could hold him all day. He smells like blintzes."

Of thee I sing.

Yankel finished rabbinical school, and the couple moved back to Crown Heights. I hardly saw my aunt anymore. When I knocked on her door, no one was home. She was always visiting the happy family.

One Sabbath, I got lucky. I found Leah in her bedroom. She was lying on her bed, tickling the child, who had grown into a small boy.

The scent of lilac entered through an open window. Next to the windowsill stood a step stool. "Look at these dimples," she said. "Did you ever see such dimples? Feel his hair, how soft." I patted his head. She went on about what a clever boy he was, climbing out of his high chair, calling her *bubbe*. She didn't even offer me a cup of tea. I didn't want to spoil the surprise I had for her, so I swallowed my anger. I had collected all the blue booklets and paid to have the lessons typed and the manuscript bound in leather. *Yiddish Lessons by Leah Masterson* was printed on the cover. I handed it to her.

I had given it to her a dozen times in my imagination. Sometimes she dropped the baby as her eyes widened and filled with tears of gratitude. Other times she took me into her arms, pressing my head to her chest.

She glanced through the pages. "Such silliness."

I closed my eyes.

"Really, Rivkah. Why waste money on such things? It's not like I made up the words."

I was about to retrieve the gift when the child stretched his hand toward the manuscript. "Look who wants to read!" Leah said. She placed the book next to him and opened it. He grabbed a page, the paper crinkling in his fist. "Such strong hands. At least someone has a use for it." Leah stood up and straightened her skirt. "*Mameleh,* watch the baby for a minute." She ducked into the bathroom.

"Good baby," I said, as he rolled onto his belly and slipped over the edge of the bed, sliding down the cotton bedspread to the floor. He tottered toward the window.

"Up?" he asked, resting his small, plump hand on the step stool.

"Up," I said. Collecting the manuscript, I dropped it into the wastebasket on my way out.

Ghost Dogs

~~~~~~~~
~~~~~

T*hwap. Thwap.* The sound of the dog door as Petal and Tanner
come and go distracts Paula as she drafts a contract on her
laptop. Dozens of laser-printed photos of the dogs spill across her desk.
She picks one up and examines it, brushes her fingers against an image of fur. Putting the photo down, she tries again to focus on her
work. It's Sunday, but Paula is desperate to catch up. Clients send
angry e-mails, demanding to know why they haven't heard from her.
She could reply, but that would only put her further behind. *Thwap.
Thwap.*

She used to hit Save, reflexively, at the end of every sentence, but
no more. It is a fallacy to think one can keep calamity at bay. Roger
programmed an automatic backup that runs weekly and will have
to do in case of crashes.

Order once governed her home office. Her desktop was immaculate except for a single photo of Roger and the dogs, and the
laptop. Now generic tea bags perch on soggy napkins. Mugs hold

three-day-old tea scum, catch crumpled tissues and contorted paper clips—an entire box unwound. The floor is an obstacle course of dog beds, squeaky toys, sterilized bones, leashes, collars, and plastic bags for picking up poop. Though it is fall, the Humane Society wall calendar is stuck on May.

The housekeeper blows through their home like a sparkling wind once a week but refuses to enter Paula's office. "I can't clean in all that mess," she says.

Thwap. Thwap. The sound is unnerving because Petal and Tanner are dead, and Roger has taken the dog door out.

Roger would rid the house of all the dog paraphernalia, box up everything for a shelter or put a carefully worded ad on Craigslist, but Paula clings to each artifact as if she believes in canine transubstantiation, that a leash will become a tail, a collar, a neck.

Heading to the kitchen for another cup of tea, Paula detours to the porch, where Roger sits in a wicker chair reading *Modern Architecture*. His frayed Columbia sweatshirt no longer swallows him. She gathers a scarf from a bench and leans in to wrap his neck, but his hand springs up to block her. Though he could sprout curls—black, sprinkled with gray—he has continued to shave his head, a look that highlights his angular cheekbones and is harsh, perhaps what he intends, a reminder to himself and others of what he has been through. Not the Roger she married, not the Roger who was sick, but someone new, someone who rubs his scalp as if discovering it.

"Don't you hear it?" she asks.

"Hear what?" His tone is flat. They have discussed the noise before.

She has a look at the back door and finds what she expects. A thin wood panel covering the dog-size hole painted by Roger, dark green to match the door. As if they could forget there was a hole. As if their eyes wouldn't always settle there.

No yellow Lab and brown Aussie jostling to get through. Once they struck the dog door simultaneously and got stuck, heads out, rumps in. Paula dropped to her knees and maneuvered Petal, the Lab, back inside. She buried her face in the dog's flank, inhaled her musty aroma, and felt as she always did in the presence of that smell, that she would never grow tired of it.

Petal, five, vaulted into strangers' truck beds. Tanner, four, anointed himself with excretions—goose, cow, horse, it didn't matter. They ate everything. Shoes, furniture, once, a set of briefs. She reported their escapades to Roger like she would those of mischievous children and took to sprinkling her possessions with pepper.

Thwap. Thwap. If their ghosts are lingering, she wants to know why. What unfinished business might dogs have?

She sets the hot mug on her desk beside two cardboard boxes. Inside each, a translucent plastic bag filled with ash and bone. She lowers a box onto her lap and opens it, feeling through the plastic to the remains. It is all she has left of Tanner, who bared his teeth at other dogs—even at Petal sometimes—and growled, guarding Paula. A dusting of ash has somehow made it to the outside of the bag, too. The dry powder coats her fingers. There are no real barriers in life. Her unhappiness blankets Roger. The dogs' energy buoyed them in the midst of his illness. She could use some of that energy now. Since they died, she's struggled to be productive. She closes the box and slides it onto the desk.

To a real-estate contract she appends contingencies: government approvals, environmental testing, loans at specified rates. Her job is to anticipate anything that might go wrong.

When she finishes the contract, Roger is in the shower. "What do you want for dinner?" she calls through the spray.

"Why don't we go out?"

She loathes the prospect of encountering someone they know and hearing Roger describe how good he feels. It doesn't make sense. She should celebrate his recovery. It isn't that she's afraid he'll jinx it. She relished nursing him, shuttling him to appointments, elevating his needs above her own. It made her feel generous and purposeful in a way racking up billable hours can't match. These days, when she helps him, she can briefly forget the dogs. She doesn't want him to die. But she wouldn't have minded if he'd stayed sick a bit longer. It's monstrous, she knows. "I thought I would just make something. We've got pork cutlets in the freezer."

"Why bother asking then?" He shouts, only in part, she suspects, to be heard above the water.

He shuts the tap and ignores the robe she holds out, reaching around her to grab a towel.

While she pounds the pork to tenderize it, she feels the dogs hovering, waiting for her to drop something into their bowls. They gained weight when Roger stopped setting them loose in the countryside because he couldn't follow behind. Petal sausaged around the middle, Tanner thickened everywhere, while Roger melted away.

"If they lose a couple of pounds, it will really extend their life spans," the vet said at the end of their last routine visit. She began running the three-mile loop around Spirit Lake with them as often as she could.

When she wakes the next morning, Roger is still asleep. He lies on his side, revealing the slashing scar across his chest. She wants to trace the scarlet line with her finger, surf its bumps and ridges, discover if it's hot or cool, but she doesn't. Since the surgery, they have barely touched each other.

Morning had been their favorite time. In the winter, still dark outside and quiet, dogs dozing on their beds in the corners of the room. With her fingertips, she would brush the small, dark moles that dot his shoulders. Register the subtle tint to his skin, reddish-tan in the dim light. Once, as they lay on their sides and held each other, they heard coyotes laughing, and Roger said, "We enjoy the sound because we lack imagination," and she understood what he meant. The coyotes' kill was invisible to them. They moved against each other as the sky purpled—the color of bruises after surgery.

Doctors proclaimed him lucky, said the position of the tumor allowed them to get it all. From other patients she learned "got it all" is a doctor's mantra, and only sometimes true. Since he was diagnosed two years ago, she has been picturing his side of the bed empty. She read somewhere that this is how actors summon tears, imagining funerals of loved ones or themselves.

Paula showers, lingering under the hot water. She runs a comb through her thin hair but doesn't style it and ignores eyeliner and blush that were once part of her morning routine, though Joyce, her paralegal, says she looks pale. A strand of Petal's fur rides Paula's black wool pantsuit. She plucks it off and adds it to her collection, depositing it in a plastic sandwich bag she keeps on her desk.

She is fifteen minutes late for her first appointment. Joyce greets her—round, heavy face puckered with worry, thick shoulders bowed. She has brought the client coffee and made conversation. "I can't stall him much longer," she whispers, as Paula drops her briefcase in her office.

Paula apologizes to the client, Barry Terwiller, who sits in the reception area, large, moisturized hands grasping the edge of the couch. He leans forward, poised, she fears, to rise on his gleaming shoes and leave. She'll be with him in a minute, she says, and then realizes she's forgotten her laptop with the real-estate contract at the house. *Fuck*. She calls Roger. He's working at home, preparing engineering drawings for the new hospital. He e-mails Joyce the contract.

Though she hasn't asked him to, Roger drops off the laptop while she's in her meeting. He reprogrammed the screensaver to say, "Lawyers do it briefly," which she realizes only after she turns the machine on in front of a client.

Her office depresses her. Just five years ago, she floated through a store, picking out the glass-topped desk shaped like a gourd, the slender ergonomic chair, the floor lamp that lights when you touch its base. It was all so modern and hopeful. Perfect for the third-floor office with views of Main Street below and cornfields beyond.

Now if it weren't for Joyce, she would labor in the semidarkness of the laptop glow, because Paula never touches the lamp or opens the shades. Joyce does that midmorning, moving nimbly, bringing a cup of tea Paula hasn't asked for but drinks. Too bad Joyce can't do anything about the files that rise in unsteady towers on the desk. A sloppy stack of loose papers conceals unanswered mail, unfiled motions. Her voice mail is full. She doesn't know where to begin.

At six, she stuffs her briefcase with work she intends to do after dinner, grabs her laptop, and heads home. Halfway there, she realizes she has forgotten to pick up Roger's blood-pressure medication.

She abhors the pharmacy, hates the false cheerfulness of the tinkling bell that greets her, the factory-scented herbal shampoos, the shelves of too-sweet candy, and most of all the medications, secured behind glass, that promise health, life even. She despises the pharmacists in their white coats, though she is not proud of that and knows it is unfair. Nothing that happened was their fault.

She can't visit the building without remembering the Saturday in early May when she stopped there on her way to take the dogs for a run at Spirit Lake.

The day began well. She and Roger had breakfast on the porch. Petal and Tanner lay at their feet, Petal licking crumbs, Tanner licking himself. Crab-apple blossoms perfumed the yard. It was hard to believe anything could be that pink. They talked about vacationing in July at famous hot springs in the southwestern part of the state. Paula's mother could watch the dogs. Even with Roger's illness, Paula had fallen only a bit behind at work.

After breakfast, Paula planted the front bed with geraniums, zinnias, and phlox, risking a hard freeze that could come as late as the end of the month. She felt confident of her luck. Roger was responding well to chemo—better than expected, the oncologist said. It looked like their lives would return to normal. That was all she wanted then.

In the afternoon, she corralled the dogs. The asphalt driveway sparkled under the midday sun. Paula waved to a neighbor swapping out a storm door for a screen. Giving winter the bird, she thought. The dogs scrambled into the back of the 4Runner. Raising her face to the sky, Paula closed her eyes and let the sun's warmth relax muscles that had been stiff with fear all winter.

As she drove, Petal and Tanner thrust their heads out the window and opened their mouths to the breeze. Jowls flapping, their exhilaration was contagious.

She stopped at the pharmacy for Roger's chemo pills and was just leaving when Peter Cornish called. "Hate to bother you, but the parcel behind my property is going on the market tomorrow. I'd like to get it under contract tonight. You think you could look at a draft in the next couple of hours?"

It was only two o'clock. There was plenty of time. She would stop by his office to pick up the document. The weather was cool enough; the dogs could stay in the car. She'd look at the contract after she got back from the run.

At his office, he got into the details: crop leases, hunting easements, loans by the seller. Occasionally, she interrupted with questions. The meeting took longer than she thought it would. When she returned to the car, the dogs were curled up in the back, asleep.

"Want to go to Spirit Lake?" Petal's tail thumped the seat. Next to her paw, the shredded white bag. Gnawed capless bottle. Not a single pill inside and none on the floor.

Stillness blanketed the car. She couldn't move though she knew she had to. The dogs looked fine. She told herself the vet would save them.

Chemo was poison even when properly administered. In small doses, a human could tolerate it. By the time she reached the vet, the medication had traveled across the dogs' stomachs and intestinal linings into their bloodstreams. There are no real barriers in life.

The vet did what he could, keeping them alive for seven days. She and Roger visited every day, feeding them roast chicken by hand, petting them through the kennel bars.

Petal died first, and as if taking a signal from her, Tanner died a few hours later. Hardly more than puppies. Paula and Roger crawled into their kennel, sat with their lifeless bodies. Paula covered herself with their ragged yellow blankets and petted them, though their hearts had stopped, her own heart having risen into her throat, beating a dull ache.

Why hadn't she put the medicine in the glove box? Or carried it into Peter's office in her purse if she didn't want him to see it? When it was over, she could think of a million ways to protect them. But she hadn't. Fucking chemo drugs, fucking cancer. She hadn't let herself feel resentment until Roger was well.

The pharmacist waves as Paula enters the drugstore. "Roger was in earlier." Of course. He picked up the drugs when he delivered her laptop.

At home, Roger has prepared dinner, a pasta and salmon salad. "I would have done that," she says.

"I'm the one who likes to cook, remember?"

She throws her suit jacket over the back of the chair. As she takes her first bite, she hears it. *Thwap. Thwap.* Roger must see her looking toward the back of the house, because he says, "I miss them, too, you know."

But it's not the same. He didn't kill them, after all. Paula remembers watching Petal in a lake, paddling, snorting, a stolen Frisbee in her mouth. When the dog emerged on the shore, her coat slick and heavy, Paula wanted to cry, she loved the dog that much. Paula rescued the toy, while Petal shook, soaking her.

"I picked up more work, doing drawings for the new elementary school."

She can tell Roger is pleased by the way he puts down his fork before making the announcement. "Do you have the energy for it?" she says.

"That's the second thing you're supposed to say. The first is congratulations."

"Congratulations."

"Too late."

As she pours water from a pitcher, ice cubes plop into her glass and splash water on the tablecloth. She blots the spill with her napkin. "You're working a lot. You're supposed to rest."

"I feel great. Doctor Peterson said to listen to my body. Being productive makes me happy. Like making dinner. You're welcome." He isn't smiling.

"Thank you."

He refills his dish from the pot on the stove but doesn't offer to refill hers.

"I'm just worried about you," she says.

"It's getting tiresome." He looks down at his plate, picks out a piece of salmon, and eats it. "I'm thinking of taking a place in town."

She stares at him, but he doesn't look up. "You're kidding."

"I'm tired of being a patient. I need to take care of myself."

"I'll let you."

"You won't. You'll hover."

"I'm sorry for caring about you."

"You could call it that."

She lifts the damp napkin, squeezes it. "I've lost the dogs, and now I'm going to lose you."

"Don't bring them into this. I saw a shrink. She said we've gotten into a pattern that's hard to break."

"You saw a shrink?" She is having trouble breathing. The same stale air, a fraction of what she needs, trickles in and out of her lungs. "When?"

"Does it matter?"

"Yes. I want to know how long you've been keeping things from me. What else haven't you told me?"

"I rented a place."

The room pulses. The appliances blur. Only Roger's calm, healthy face is clear. She would like to strike it, but she can't rise from the chair or lift her arms. She is paralyzed.

"It's furnished, so I don't have to move anything out. Just take some clothes. It will be good for you, too. You can focus on your practice. Catch up."

She doesn't think anything she says will matter. "I'm keeping their ashes."

He rises from the table. She follows him through the house as he packs a large bag, clothes for several seasons. He places the essentials of his office in cardboard boxes he must have gathered earlier and carries the boxes to his truck. From her desk, he takes a picture of the dogs but none of her.

Awake most of the night, she thinks how unfair it is that he left her after she took care of him. Though she has no reason for suspicion, she wonders if he met someone else. She remembers going to the shelter with Roger to adopt Petal, how excited they were to enlarge their family, to share the affection they had for each other, which seemed boundless.

The following day, Roger calls her at work to say he'll be at the house that afternoon. She breathes deeply for the first time since he left, thinking he's coming home, but then he says he just needs to pick up a few more things.

In bed that night, she turns on a reality television program in which drunken housewives scream at each other and throw punches.

The show makes her feel sane, and she watches it for hours. When she finally turns the television off, the silence is oppressive. She stares at the photograph she relocated to the nightstand, of Roger and the dogs. How has she lost everything she loves? A tidal wave separated her from the best parts of her life, and she is that wave.

~~~~~~~~~~

A week later, Joyce brings tea and says they ought to celebrate by going to lunch. "I'm not sure if you realize, but it's the fifth anniversary of the firm. November tenth. I know because it's the day I started."

"I don't feel like celebrating. Maybe another time." Paula stands and walks to the door, hoping Joyce will take the hint and follow, but she moves slowly because she likes hearing Joyce's voice.

"I've always wanted to tell you this," Joyce says, sitting in the chair opposite the desk. "I don't know why I never did. You saved my life. I'd gone on a million interviews, and no one hired me. No one said why, but I knew. I've been facing it all my life. People see a big woman and think I'm stupid or lazy or both. I was down to my last month's rent."

When Paula first met Joyce, she thought the paralegal's open face and clear eyes would put clients at ease. Paula feels awkward standing by the door, addressing Joyce's back, so she returns to her chair and grasps the handle of the fresh mug of tea. With the fingertips of her other hand, she strokes the cup's glazed surface, lightly, to avoid burning herself. "I know what you're trying to do, and I appreciate it."

"You don't know. If this practice fails, I'll be looking again, and maybe I'll find something, and maybe I won't." She wipes her temple with the side of her index finger.

Until now, Paula hasn't noticed Joyce's distress, so well hidden behind self-reliance and efficiency. Focused on her own unraveling life, Paula hasn't considered that the paralegal is counting on her to keep the law practice alive, and that she, Paula, is failing not only herself and her clients, but Joyce, too. She would like to take care of Joyce, who has always taken care of her. But when she looks at her desk, the backlog seems to have grown, and she feels powerless to get it under control.

A month later, Paula's in the pharmacy, picking up the St. John's Wort that Joyce recommended. Avoiding the back where the drugs are kept, she sees Roger in front. He's still bald and looks stronger, as if he's been working out. He turns and sees her. Stepping out of the cash-register line, he approaches her, and Paula feels excited. Maybe he's had enough of their separation.

He tells her the county has hired him to work on the courthouse expansion.

She says, "Congratulations."

He says, "Thanks." There's a condo he wants to buy. He lowers his voice and says his lawyer will call. That is how she learns her marriage is over. Though it ended the day she left Petal and Tanner in the car with the chemo, killing the dogs as she tried to save Roger.

Thwap, thwap, she hears that night as she carries dirty teacups into her kitchen. *Thwap, thwap,* as she dumps their contents into the trash. Perhaps she can trick the pain by staying busy. Nothing else has worked. She wasn't expecting Roger's news, but she should have been. She might have braced herself for it.

Selecting a picture of Tanner and one of Petal from the many on her desk, she slides them into frames she emptied of photos of her and Roger. The rest of the photos—of the dogs and Roger—she layers in a shoebox.

She bags dog beds, toys, sterilized bones. As she packs leashes, she hears it again, louder this time and more urgent, heartbreaking and haunting, and she finally understands. She promised to run with them that Saturday in May; they are still stuck, waiting.

Acknowledgments

My deepest thanks to my editor, Deb Futter, for incorporating my dream of a collection of stories into her vision for a new publishing family at Celadon Books. Her support and the support of the entire Celadon team have exceeded my hopes.

My agent, Victoria Sanders, is a magician who took a chance on my collection and on me as a writer. Agents Bernadette Baker-Baughman and Jessica Spivey at VSA helped lead me through the sale of my first books, graciously answering questions and calming my anxieties.

I couldn't have written this collection without the help of Will Allison and Erika Krouse, whose deeply thoughtful critiques guided me. As I drafted the stories, I had the privilege of studying the craft of fiction with Laura Pritchett and Clare Beams, and workshop leaders Jill McCorkle and Steve Yarbrough at the Sewanee Writers' Conference, Ursula Hegi at the Bread Loaf Writers' Conference, and

Rebecca Makkai, Robin Black, and Antonya Nelson at Lighthouse Writers Workshop. I hear your wisdom as I work.

Literary magazine editors Halimah Marcus, Maegan Poland, Lorinda Toledo-Smailes, and Suzanne McConnell first published several of the stories with such great care.

Friends who encouraged me to dream on paper, who read and guided my work: Hilary Zaid, Melissa Scholes Young, Wendi Temkin, Laura Smith, Shoney Sien, Natalie Serber, Lia Pripstein, Heidi Pate, Drea Knufken, Kathy Kaiser, Emily Franklin, Linda Cornett, Kathy Conde, Elissa Cahn, and fellow writers at Bread Loaf, Sewanee, Lighthouse, and the AWP Writer to Writer Mentorship Program, especially my mentor, Jon Papernick. I don't know where I would be without all of you.

Many thanks to my mother, Hannah Maizes, of blessed memory, who, whenever I complained I was bored, responded, "Read a book!" My father, Isaac Maizes, was never without a book in his hand. My sisters, Beth, Victoria, and Miriam, not only read drafts of my work but also know where I come from. Your friendship is a gift.

I've been told it's going overboard to mention the animals who have traveled alongside me, teaching me about love, giving me comfort, and serving as muses. Sorry, Tilly, Chance, Molly, Flora, Arie, and Rosie. That's just how it goes.

Finally, to my husband, Steve, whose love sustains me: We found each other just in time. Hold on tight.

About the Author

Adrianne Mathiowetz

R.L. Maizes was born and raised in Queens, New York, and now lives in Boulder County, Colorado. Maizes's short stories have aired on National Public Radio and have appeared in the literary magazines *Electric Literature, Witness, Bellevue Literary Review, Slice,* and *Blackbird,* among others. Her essays have been published in *The New York Times, The Washington Post, Lilith,* and elsewhere.

Maizes is an alumna of the Bread Loaf Writers' Conference, the Sewanee Writers' Conference, and the Tin House Summer Writer's Workshop. Her work has received Honorable Mention in Glimmer Train's Fiction Open contest, has been a finalist in numerous other national contests, and has been nominated for a Pushcart Prize. *We Love Anderson Cooper* is her first book.

CELADON
BOOKS

Founded in 2017, Celadon Books, a division of
Macmillan Publishers, publishes a highly curated
list of twenty to twenty-five new titles a year. The
list of both fiction and nonfiction is eclectic and
focuses on publishing commercial and literary
books and discovering and nurturing talent.